CostaLiving
Laughing through life

by
PETER COSTA

Copyright © 2006
Peter Costa

All rights reserved. No part of this publication may be reproduced, stored in a retrieval system, or transmitted in any form or by any means, electronic, mechanical, photocopying, recording, or otherwise, without the prior written permission of the author/publisher. All of the pieces in this book appeared in slightly different form in the Westford Eagle published by the Community Newspaper Company.

Library of Congress Control Number: 2006903638
ISBN 0-9785068-0-4

Printed in the U.S.A. by
Morris Publishing
3212 East Highway 30
Kearney, NE 68847
1-800-650-7888

Acknowledgements

I would like to thank Kathleen Cordeiro, Editor In Chief of the Northwest unit of the Community Newspaper Company, for granting me a weekly forum for my CostaLiving columns. Ray Johnson designed this book and has been the driving force behind the design of the individual CostaLiving columns. Jesse Floyd, Carrie Simmons and Ariel Z. Burch were responsible for proofreading my columns, so send any typographical error notifications, or evidence of grammatical barbarisms, to them. Holly Camero helped collect these columns.

Finally, I want to thank my wife, Sara, and my daughter, Lucy, for putting up with me over the decades as I chased down my own stories, edited those of others and wrote my commentaries. They also have shown true grace and remarkable patience for answering my persistent question, "Well, what do you think of the piece?" with the response: "It's funny, Peter, very funny," even though it wasn't that funny.

The New England Press Association presented me with humor columnist awards for two consecutive years. Praise from one's peers is worth more than money – especially when writers don't get any real money in the first place.

Finally, I would like to acknowledge all those readers who sent me an e-mail, wrote a letter, telephoned kind words, submitted a ransom note or left voice mail that contained veiled legal threats.

You keep me on my toes.

Peter Costa
March 2006

Contents

1. On suffering colds — almost in silence
2. Lions are from Mars, Elephants are from Venus
3. Slouching toward the DNC
4. Shedding light on our armchair obsessions
5. Making press deadline, it's by its
6. Putting out a newspaper – Part 2
7. There's gold in them-thar pipes
8. It's the image thing, Mr. President
9. Super Bowl XL: Mick enters the Stone Age
10. Help, I'm being held against my will in e-mail jail
11. What did you do this holiday weekend, anything fun?
12. Working with Grace under pressure
13. My word(s), what's a glove box?
14. Trolling for a fishing license
15. My PC is a Fatal Error
16. Fall: Wet leaves, clanging furnaces and sidewalk sand
17. Dry-gulched at the dry cleaners
18. Let them eat cake and donuts
19. 'Down talkers' can really ruin your day
20. Gamut, gauntlet, Madonna, Sting
21. Google eavesdropping: Search or search and seizure
22. Dieting, Dr. Atkins and Patti Hearst
23. On CV joint repair and surviving auto repair waiting rooms
24. The tale of two couches
25. Fluent in the shop talk of public safety
26. Road not taken: stomach crunches
27. Bee Gees and words are all we have
28. On wiper blades, mechanics and the grammar of life
29. On buying gifts for the holidays
30. Winter sport: battery jump starting
31. Clowns, columns and Art Hoppe
32. On gasoline prices and giant vehicles
33. Summertime and the grilling isn't easy

Contents

34. Splendor in the grass
35. Life in the failed lane
36. Rockets red glare and other work-related noises
37. Procrastination: Wait, wait don't tell me
38. Path of Least Resistance resolutions
39. Language that passes muster
40. Car repair bill like ransom note
41. For some, the silence of early retirement is unbearable
42. Stream of consciousness overflows its banks
43. Reporting the news, phrase by phrase
44. Beware 'sunny' Ides of March
45. Thanksgiving: gambits among the giblets
46. Right tool for right job — somewhere
47. Surviving a world without work
48. Ruminations on being the man in a van
49. To have and to hold, every 3,000 miles
50. On spring and a weighty wharf
51. It's OK to be wicked smart
52. 'Work deco' adorns cubicles
53. Return to sender: Bragging holiday cards
54. Young and old: MP3 versus Timex
55. The weather: rain, raw, ridiculous
56. Of leaves, rakes and chiropractors
57. Taking stock after the holiday
58. April, and cruel blades of grass
59. Understanding nuances of snow blower etiquette
60. CO monitor installation can make you dizzy
61. Well, partners, time to saddle up for spring
62. When trying to fall asleep is but a dream
63. Ne'er-do-wells of American usage
64. Charlie and the power of pookies
65. Is Dave Barry hyphenated?

1.

ON SUFFERING COLDS — ALMOST IN SILENCE

I have a cold. Actually, I have what my mother would have called a "head cold." The symptoms of a head cold are runny nose, watery eyes, sneezing and congestion. The worst symptom of a bad head cold is a low-grade fever that causes me to have a chill even while wearing a chamois shirt and huddled under a blanket.

I should also admit that I am a lousy patient. I sigh a lot when I am sick. Sometimes I moan. Other times I say to my wife: "I am really sick this time." Or, my favorite utterance, said in the somber tone of a Supreme Court Chief Justice issuing a ruling, is: "I am not well."

Now, you need to understand that if there were an Olympic class for stoics, my wife would be its team captain. The only time I might get her sympathy is for a gunshot wound. But it would have to be a non-self-inflicted gunshot wound. Then, she might say, "OK, maybe we should stop the bleeding and have someone sew you up."

For a head cold her therapy of choice is studied avoidance. Not only is a head cold trivial in her world in which Spartan warriors would be considered namby-pamby wimps, but it is absurd to mention even having a cold if you are an adult. You simply suffer it in silence. Period. Anything else is unbecoming.

Even after all these years of marriage, I must say that my wife's Vulcan bedside manner still troubles me. You see, I was horribly spoiled by my emotional, Captain Kirk of a mother. When I was sick as a boy, my Mom would rub my chest with Vicks Vapo Rub, heat up a glass of ginger ale for me and serve me some cookies she had just made. If I had a fever, she would sit at my bedside and place a cool wash cloth on my forehead. If I were coughing a lot, she would spoon feed me cherry-flavored cough medicine, which I now realize, must have had the alcohol content of a bottle of stiff sherry.

When her friends would call her on our big black telephone with the rotary dial (only important calls were made back then, calls inquiring about one's health, for example), she would say: "Peter, is quite sick." Quite sick. It was a validation of my suffering.

Often she would read to me from "My Book House," a collection of 12 or so volumes of stories from fairy tales for toddlers to the epic "Song of Roland," illustrated with beautifully drawn color figures. The illustration of a Bengal tiger still triggers an occasional nightmare to this day.

But instead of "My Book House," I now get "The Compete Book of Symptoms, A Self-Help Guide." I read this text carefully, checking for all the signs of sickness and reading aloud the ones that sound the most potentially life-threatening. But none of this sways my wife, the care-giver. "Take more Tylenol," she says as dispassionately as if she were reading the periodic chart of the elements.

I do as she says. I try to sigh less. I drink as many fluids as possible, enough to burst the Hoover Dam, and still my chills continue, my eyes hurt and I am on my second box of man-sized tissues.

Is there any ginger ale in the house? How about cookies? No?

I am not well.

2.

Lions are from Mars, Elephants are from Venus

Ruling the jungle is gender-biased. The male lion, simply by being bigger than female lions and by being a fierce meat-eating predator, is called the king of the jungle. We think the female elephant, who rules her herd and who has no physical equal in the land-animal world, should be king, or more accurately, queen of the jungle.

The toughest male lion dominates his group, which is technically known as a "pride" of lions. How appropriate a name pride is for a group of macho ruffians. Females wear the trunks in the elephant family. In fact, male bull elephants are forced to hang out in separate bachelor bands away from the group of ruling females.

The wisest and oldest female elephant guides the heard to feeding grounds and remembers where water holes are, what dangers lie ahead, who usually behaves along the way and who does not. She usually runs the herd with the help of her sisters, daughters and cousins and only calls upon the male elephants when the female herd is threatened or when she thinks it is time for the females to mate.

Male elephants, especially when they are filled with a substance similar to testosterone called, musk, are pretty useless, rowdy and out of control most of the time. They push each other around and bulldoze trees with their trunks and exhibit typically male locker room behavior.

But when they get the call from the ruling female, who promises the males access to the females if they rush over to rescue the herd from any danger, like a pride of lions growling at them, well, then, they zoom on over.

Pity anything that gets in the way of a bunch of big bull elephants running to the aid of their potential mates and the rewards they anticipate. Bull elephants have been known to level villages, push down walls and overturn LandRovers and 4-wheel-drive trucks as if they were thimbles.

Lions prey on other animals; elephants are vegetarians. Elephants have no known predators, except for humans with guns. Lions pose and preen a lot, growl, fight, mark their territories and jump out from tall grass to attack any mammal that moves.

Elephants stay in a group and chat. They are, like the stereotype of traditional women, "relational." They don't threaten other animals, only flowers and fruit trees, which they find particularly yummy.

They are very social. Elephants value the family. They grieve for lost ones and help comfort each other during crises.

The legends about elephants having long memories, especially when it comes to family members, are apparently validated by scientific studies. Take this case, for example. Two female cousin elephants, who worked in a circus together, were separated. One of the elephants had been sold to another circus. Eventually after 23 years, they were reunited. They immediately recognized each other and spent the next five days sniffing each other's hides to obtain an olfactory archaeology of where each had been for the past two decades. After the five days, the elephant who had been gone for 23 years rejoined the main herd and resumed her place amid her nieces and cousins as if she had never left.

Lions seem only to remember their last meal. They eat a lot, take naps, growl and prance around the savanna. But they are scary and menacing to humans and other animals. Perhaps that is why, fearful humans bestow the kingship on them, instead of on the keep-to-themselves, vegetarian, gentle-unless-disturbed, giant elephants. (Zoologists say it is amazing how softly an elephant can walk. It is unnerving to be seated at your campfire and to turn around and see that you have been silently joined by a seven-ton, 13-foot-high elephant looking over your shoulder intrigued by the smell of the coffee you are brewing.)

Yet, despite their generally gregarious group behavior, if there were a fight between a pride of lions and a herd of angry elephants, elephants can get down and dirty. Elephants have been known to dispatch a pesky lion either by a single piercing thrust of their tusks or by stepping on the lion's back crushing it. In some cases, an elephant merely picks up an attacking lion with its trunk and tosses it against a stout tree.

(It is true, unfortunately, that sometimes a very sick elephant, or a baby separated from the herd, cannot defend itself against a pride of lions and often one hears of an elephant being eaten by carnivores. But for the most part, they live to an old age (around 70) and die of natural causes, usually after their last set of molars wear out and they can no longer eat the 300-500 pounds of vegetation they require each day.).

Among the powerful land animals, the elephant is clearly peerless.

So, let's dethrone the lion king, and elevate the elephant. Long may she rule.

3.

SLOUCHING TOWARD THE DNC

People are dreading driving into Boston during the Democratic National Convention. I think they are worrying unnecessarily.

Just because the convention is located in the middle of the Big Dig where search teams are still looking for seven cement-mixers last seen near potholes in the Central Artery in 2001, and just because a security zone blast area larger in circumference than the Great Wall of China has been established around the FleetCenter, there is no need to get emotionally overheated. Yes, traffic experts are predicting roadway tie-ups so lengthy that male motorists will have to shave twice en route to the office in the morning.

And yes, there are studies that indicate the convention will paralyze greater Boston and the adjoining states of New Hampshire and Maine. Connecticut is going to be just fine - at least south of Hartford. And even if the Nutmeg State suffers, they deserve it for rooting for the Yankees. (Vermont is part of New York anyway and doesn't figure in anything east of the Lee tollbooth on the Mass Turnpike.)

But why the despair? The convention will last only four days. Think of it as merely four days without oxygen. Or, what doesn't make you stronger, can kill you.

You will be able to tell your grandchildren that in '04 you spent 6 hours waiting through 74 light cycles before you could cross an intersection in Woburn. You can tell them about the hapless couple from Saco, Maine who were discovered in a one-way grid in South Boston and who resorted to tenant farming to try to survive until the traffic detours were removed.

But not everyone will suffer. AM radio talk show hosts are ecstatic about having an on-road audience they can preach to for 96 nonstop hours. The company that produces Valium is watching its stock price reach stratospheric levels. The black market in gasoline is rivaling stolen diamonds.

But if you think it is going to be challenging outside the FleetCenter, inside the convention promises to reach psychic depths heretofore reached only by Jules Verne in the first Nautilus. Just think about the Congressman from the 19th district in Iowa who has been chosen to read the platform plank on improving product labeling to a yawning audience at 10:45 a.m. on a Tuesday. Or the secretary of the convention taking the roll of states who support the plank on decreasing downwind air particulates from 6 parts per million to 5 parts per million, where applicable and where such an imposition of said new regulation does not lower present levels of employment in traditional smoke-stack industries.

You will also see NBC's Tom Brokaw striding across the floor of the convention hall getting the incredible scoop over his two competitor anchormen that the honorable state of West Virginia will give one of its votes to honor its senior senator, the venerable Robert Byrd. Dan Rather will use his Texas connections to learn when the Lone Star state will vote unanimously to memorialize the heroes of the Alamo with a proclamation read from the podium of the great hall. Peter Jenkins, the only anchorman who is Canadian, will explain how the U.S. convention process works and how smart our forefathers were in coming up with such an open forum for choosing one's party's presidential ticket.

The Democrats will have considerable difficulty maintaining elements of mystery and drama. We already know who the presidential candidate is. We know who his running mate is. The only thing left to chance is whether someone will make an incredible gaff. And someone almost always does.

So, we look forward to driving and driving in our vehicles those four fateful days and to hearing Mayor Menino at the end of the four days tell us how grateful he is that everything turned out so well. Let's hope so.

Soon we all can return to the remains of the Big Dig and the daily rollovers on I-93 and get ready to watch the anchormen descend on the Republicans in the Big Apple.

The interesting thing about that convention is that New York City anticipates no change in traffic tie-ups at all. The 4-hour delay on the George Washington Bridge will still be 4 hours.

4.
SHEDDING LIGHT ON OUR ARMCHAIR OBSESSIONS

Why is it that the investigators on the television show, "CSI," always examine the crime scene by flashlight? Does Las Vegas suffer from one long, continuous blackout? Even at high noon, you can see Willows or Grissom looking for "voids" or "blood splatter" on walls with their Maglite® flashlights - those are the ones with the rotating lens we all get for Christmas from our nephews.

In fact, if you remember "The X-Files" with Scully and Mulder, they too always seemed to be entering rooms holding flashlights. Of course, in their show, which dealt with crimes as they happened, they drew their guns and illuminated potential targets with their Maglites® held just above their gun barrels. I guess it is true that crime does occur mostly at night and that's why we hear the expression of astonishment when a crime is committed "in broad daylight." (What is narrow daylight?)

A cynic might also say that it is cheaper to film things when your main characters are seen using flashlights because then one does not have to do much set design. Black is black, night is night and the viewer's imagination becomes the set designer.

Another thing I notice about television is that all car commercials not filmed on the 30,000-acre Bonneville Salt Flats are filmed in the city with the cars zooming over wet roadways. Art directors love the way wet pavement reflects the light and gives the shot a satin patina. Movie directors also like streets to be wet when they shoot a scene. They even go so far as to hire the local fire pumper truck to come out and wet down the streets in Toronto where most American films seem to be filmed.

Also, have you ever noticed in cowboy Western movies on TV that the wagon wheels on the stage coach always seem to be spinning backward? I once asked a physicist to explain this phenomenon and he said something about a stroboscopic effect caused by the slow sampling frame rate of 16 millimeter film. I didn't have the courage to say, "Hey, I still don't understand it; try telling me again."

If you listen closely enough to your TV, when a superimposed graphic or title is shown on the bottom of your screen, the sound changes and sounds fuzzy ever so slightly. Ever notice how Tom Brokaw rocks a bit when he delivers the news while standing? I thought humans only had 32 teeth. How come Paula Zahn has 36? Do people cry on camera for Barbara Walters because they are moved by her insightful questions or because they wish they had never granted the interview to someone who asks what kind of tree they are? The only one who speaks faster than "Washington Week" moderator Gwen Ifill when she is wound up on some Beltway topic is the fast-talking "small print" readers on car commercials - "price does not include dealer prep, destination charges, etc."

The most clever things on television are not the shows but the commercials. How do these people think of these incredibly funny things? The Nextel Perfect Pittsburgh Paper commercial, where executives sit around a conference table discussing via walkie-talkie cell phone the moving of their plant, comes to mind.

Success on television means spin-offs. If one format succeeds, make as many versions of it as you can. There is "CSI," "CSI-Miami," and "Navy NCIS." What's next, "CSI-Brockton?"

How about a show called, "The Bachelor Dates Survivors Who Have No Fear Factor And Who Have An Alias And Work For CSI?" The only thing we have to make sure is that the Bachelor should examine his possible mates with a flashlight.

5.

MAKING PRESS DEADLINE, IT'S BY ITS

I am often asked to write about what it is like to put out a newspaper.

Well, I wear a gray business suit with wide lapels and a fedora hat. My only disguise is a pair of black-rimmed eyeglasses that seem to fool my newsroom colleague, Lois Lane, all the time. When I have to save people, I run down an alley and change into my superhero's suit and cape, and if I haven't hit the donut tray too often that morning in the newsroom, I jog down the alley until I reach takeoff speed and fly off into thin air.

Of course, I have lots of help from photographer Jimmy Olsen and our editor "don't-call-me-chief" Perry White. And, yes, I talk over story ideas with Lois, virtually all day long.

But, alas, that's how it is done on The Daily Planet. For a local newspaper, it's different.

I get to work, literally before sunrise, and log onto our computer network. Booting up the computer is agonizingly long when you have lived a lifetime of deadlines. This waiting especially frustrates me when I've got a lead I want to write to a story that will bust the town wide open - as they used to say in the 1930s. Finally, the system comes up, Word opens, and it is hoped, ideas and stories flow down.

The next thing I do is check the e-mail. Now, even though our company has installed so-called "spam" filters, we receive hundreds of messages that urge us to buy products to enlarge certain body parts or other products that promise to reduce our mortgage payments. Many messages are offers for spam filters, which is doubly ironic: Getting spam telling us how to avoid spam.

Hidden in the spam are notes and press releases from legitimate news sources, ranging from cub scout packs to the state Supreme Court. Even the W's West Wing staffers send us press releases with information about the economy, the Pentagon, etc.

Once we have separated out the truly useful stories from the dross, we have to edit them to fit the approved newspaper style and format.

Editing consumes the largest amount of our time - more than even attending meetings, interviewing sources and writing stories. While T.S. Eliot complained about measuring out his life in coffee spoons, I measure my life by the hours I spend changing `PM' to p.m.

Many newspapers institute rules of spelling, usage and style to ensure the prose they publish is uniform and consistent. Newspapers generally abide by the rules of an approved "stylebook."

We use the Associated Press Stylebook as our first reference but we also consult an in-house, companion stylebook compiled by Community Newspaper Company editors, which has several local usage and style preferences. (*Borders Book Shop* — no apostrophe; *FleetCenter* — one word.)

The wire service stylebook has an interesting history. In the late 1970s and early 1980s, the two wire services, the AP and United Press International, teamed up and came out with a joint stylebook. The stylebook committee members, who met in New York City, had long and spirited debates about how words should be spelled and used.

Battles erupted over whether the proper way to write *1960s* was *1960s* or *1960's*. (They ruled *1960s*. The New York Times, however, which always seems to march to its own drummer, uses *1960's*.) The word, *judgment*, lost an "e" in those wire service deliberations. The adjective, *full-time*, gained a hyphen.

Why does a newspaper bother? Well, the primary reason to follow AP style is to make sure the local copy, written and edited by the newspaper staff, follows the same rules as the state, national and international copy provided by the wire service. Because wire service copy often appears side-by-side with local copy in the newspaper, editors believe all copy should adhere to the same rules.

Despite that proviso, some reporters and correspondents are about as familiar with AP style as they are with the Rosetta Stone. They turn in copy that might as well have been written in Klingon and boldly go into typographical worlds where no editor has gone before. They jar editors awake by suddenly throwing in a series of *!!!*, which is the equivalent of shouting in print. Or, they will say something will occur at *9:00PM* on Tuesday night, instead of 9 *p.m. Tuesday.* (Night is redundant; one only uses a colon after the hour number to indicate minutes, as in 9:30 p.m. Otherwise it's 9 p.m.)

Speaking of it's: This is perhaps the most-common mistake made by young and old journalists. Here is the entry in the AP Stylebook for the difference:

It's, its

It's is a contraction for *it is* or *it has*. *It's up to you. It's been a long time.*

Its is the possessive form of the neuter pronoun: *The company lost its assets.*

I try to tell reporters, correspondents and students to think of *its* like *hers*. The lipstick was *hers*. Then, I confuse them with a sample sentence like the following: *It's hers; put it back.* (I'm such a smart aleck.)

OK, now I hope I made my point that putting the prose in appropriate style is not trivial, as the mathematicians are wont to say. (Do you know how many p.m.'s there are in a typical column listing events? Hundreds.)

Once the copy is edited for style, it has to be looked at for its storytelling aspects as well as for libel.

An aside: Many times, we receive letters inveighing against a person that, if published, run the risk of defaming a person without giving him or her a chance to rebut or refute the allegations. Often, some of the language in the letters has the potential to injure a person's reputation. Let's look at the definition of libel provided in the AP Stylebook:

> *Words, pictures or cartoons that expose a person to public hatred, shame, disgrace or ridicule or induce an ill opinion of a person is libelous.*

That is why we do not run letters that meet any of the above conditions.

OK, enough for how we start the typical newspaper morning. In next week's column, I will try to show how we survive the afternoons.

6.

PUTTING OUT A NEWSPAPER — PART 2

After rewriting, editing and formatting the copy, and after having have had enough coffee to defibrillate a fallen wildebeest, then it is time for the editor to decide where to place the stories and photos in the paper.

This function, in newspaper parlance, is called layout. This is not to be confused with guys packing heat who meet in a hotel with Bogey and ask: "What's the layout, boss?" Layout is an art form that requires accurate measurements, planning and a design sense. Most editors are masters of at least one of these three areas — usually, the first. We can measure copy beautifully because our personal computers are equipped with a feature that automatically determines the length of a story with one keystroke command. Voila: the story is 24 inches long.

The other two skill sets — planning and design — are more difficult to acquire. The really good designers eventually leave the editor ranks and become Web designers or work for Donna Karen in New York. The planners remain editors and continue to put out pages that look professional but seldom rise above the level of good-looking wallpaper.

Once the stories are measured for length, space must be found for them. Determining which story gets the larger headline and which appears higher up on the page relates to the importance of the story to the readership, the news value of the story, the quality of the writing, and whether it is accompanied by "art." By art, we mean photos or illustrations.

Now let us be clear that our photography department does not like the word "art." Nor do they like it when we ask them if they have time from their schedules to "shoot" a picture for us. They don't shoot pictures, I am told daily; rather, they compose an image. When looking at a photograph provided by one of their colleagues, they often say things, like, "Yeah, that's a great image." This I find confusing, because I think of image as something one creates by doing something cool for a long time, as in: "She projects a very-caring image."

Nonetheless, the photojournalists in our company compose the image and then print out a color paper copy of it for us to include with our layout sheets. Once we see the photos that we have to illustrate the story, we decide how to package the story and photo on a page.

Generally speaking, the most important story gets the largest headline and is allotted the greatest space on a page.

A few words about headline writing: This too is a skill and sometimes writing a clever headline can get the reader to read an otherwise run-of-the-mill story. One of the most famous headlines was written when New York City was in grave fiscal straits and sought a bailout from then-President Gerald Ford. He declined to float federal bonds to save New York City. The next morning the New York Daily News sported the following headline, the top line in medium-sized type, the second line in billboard-sized type:

Ford to city:
Drop Dead

So, most editors try to write a headline that is catchy and punchy. This usually requires a command of muscular verbs. (An aside: if I were in the West in the 1880s, I would steal a line from Paladin's business card and change it slightly to read: Have verbs; will travel. Or, today, if I had my own business and were a *man in a van*, I would go to the job site with a tool belt filled with active verbs and would keep going back to the van to file and sharpen a verb to install in my customer's prose.)

So armed with verbs like *deny, endorse, strike* and *plummet*, we cast our headline. Then, we size the photo. This operation requires a sense of proportion – literally. Most photos have to be reduced in size to fit on a page. Sizing photos requires the following proportion: original width is to desired width as original depth is to reduced depth. (The only variable the editor does not know and has to calculate is reduced depth.)

Now, one can do this arithmetical function on a calculator or in your head if you had starred in your high school's play, "Revenge of the Nerds," or you can use what we call a "proportional wheel.' This is a neat circular slide-rule type device that figures out the fractions for you. I like using the wheel because I think it makes me look like Merlin, or more historically accurate, Pythagoras who had a passion for numbers and their combinations/permutations. Does the 3-4-5 triangle, ring any bells?

So, we have sized the photos and written the headlines. Now, we enter those two elements on a large paper layout grid that we will eventually hand over to our team of paginators who work on jumbo-screened Macintosh computers. (All "real" design people love Macs; they hate IBM boxes.)

Then, we move on to the next page. Oh, by the way, the pages come to us with ads on them. What is left of the space on the page is called the "news hole." That is where we place news stories and photos. The news hole is directly proportional to the number of ads sold. The more ads, the greater the news hole.

So, we work page by page through the paper, writing headlines, sizing photos, filling up the news hole. One question I get all the time, from grade-schoolers and grandmothers alike, is: How come the news fits exactly every week. Well, it doesn't. Sometimes we enlarge a photo to fill a few lines of white space or shrink a photo to get all the copy on the page.

Other times we will drop a visual element from the layout like the logo of the police or fire badge on the For the Record page, for example. Sometimes, if the story is a few lines long, we will trim a few sentences from the bottom of a news story. News stories are usually written with the most important information in the first few paragraphs and information of lesser importance falls toward the end, or falls off, the end.

So after the last page goes to the paginators, they flow all the elements onto their screens electronically, move it here and there, and then send it over our wired network to our printer in an inky galaxy far away. The printer converts the digital information into aluminum sheets, which are bolted on a rotary printing press. Then someone presses a large red button that fires a claxon horn warning the press people to step away from the press and the press starts. Long continuous rolls of newsprint unfold and feed into the ink-laden rollers of the press. The newsprint streams through the rollers and comes out in sections and "the folder" part of the press cuts them into newspapers.

A few hours later, boys on bikes throw them in the vicinity of your house. By that time, I am again collecting a bunch of PMs to change into p.m.'s and starting another work week.

7.

THERE'S GOLD IN THEM-THAR PIPES

Looking for salary justice is an exercise in futility that goes beyond the economics of simple supply and demand.

I just cannot seem to let go of the fact that people who control water earn more money than people who control blood.

A master plumber often earns more than a master heart surgeon. An average house call by a plumber ranges from $150 to $400 for no more than an hour or two of work. So that amounts to about $5,000 to $7,500 per week or $260,000 to $390,000 per year. (Yes, I know that there are many heart surgeons who are millionaires; there are thousands, however, who are not and earn less than plumbers.)

Now, granted, plumbers, unlike doctors, make house calls because one cannot bring the house to the plumber but one has to bring the patient to the hospital. So plumbers have to figure in travel time to the job site, wear and tear on their vans, vehicle insurance, etc. The surgeon also has built-in costs: malpractice insurance, wear and tear on his scalpels, batteries for the pacemakers, etc.

But seriously, all in all, when you estimate the earning potentials of plumbers versus surgeons, the plumbers win. Even though plumbers have to apprentice for a few years, their training pales when compared to medical school, residency and the post-medical school training a surgeon requires to become board certified.

But I am not merely picking on plumbers. I also object to the auto repair industry that charges on average $300 to $800 for a single repair. Their fees are too high but we seem not to have any recourse but to pay them.

Others claim that at least plumbers and auto technicians provide something tangible and useful whereas other extremely highly paid people provide something less tangible. Take rock stars, TV anchormen, entertainers, baseball players and lobbyists, all of whom earn a Pharaoh's wages and don't have to worry about the wheat crop failing and having their subjects depose them in a swift, angry, hungry coup.

As a newspaperman, I write this out of sheer, unvarnished envy.

When it comes to money, working for a newspaper ranks below custodial work. We like to think that we perform a useful function in the democracy by informing citizens of what is going on in their world. Some journalists also cherish the perk of knowing something before anyone else does. We are also authorized to come back to the fire and tell a story interesting enough to make some one think, smile, cry or leave the cave.

Teachers have a similar mission. Even though they earn so little, sometimes only $32,000 a year even with a Ph.D. degree and 30 years of experience, some teachers take solace in the fact they are helping their students live productive and meaningful lives as educated citizens. Someone once said that teaching is like being a part of infinity - teachers' students go out in the world and interact with others based on what their teachers taught them and they then teach their children and their children eventually teach others. Former students thus bend the space-time social continuum in ways their teachers often cannot envision. That feeling is something that money cannot buy.

Looking for salary justice is an exercise in futility that goes beyond the economics of simple supply and demand.

Maybe the answer is to put down the T.S. Eliot and pick up a propane torch on the weekends. Imagine scores of poet-plumbers, reciting the line that they measured out their lives in coffee spoons as they lie underneath kitchen sinks across America, solder in hand with a van outside filled with gold.

8.

It's the Image Thing, Mr. President

In the image-driven, bumper-sticker, sound-bite world of presidential politics, the photo op rules.

Perhaps that explains why our presidents do things for the camera that later seem so incredibly inadvisable.

Take Richard Nixon, for example. Remember his two-arm, overhead wave good-bye with his fingers forming V's for victory s à la Winston Churchill ("Win one for Winnie") from the door of his helicopter as he was to leave the White House, the first president in history to resign?

Or how about Clinton's saxophone playing while wearing sunglasses on the Arsenio Hall Show? (His swinger image may actually have been closer to the truth than his handlers would ever have thought – especially for someone who knows the meaning of the word "is.")

Then there is the hapless President Ford slicing a golf ball into a crowd of terrified onlookers or President Ford tripping down the steps of Air Force One. Thank goodness Ford knew how to hit the ground and roll with it from his college football days.

Or how about President Bush, the elder, looking at his wristwatch during one of the presidential debates as if he had somewhere else better to be than telling the voters how he plans to rule? This was the same president for whom the White House scheduled hundreds of photo ops off the coast of Kinnebunkport where the "I'm no wimp" president churned up the waters with his Miami Vice cigarette-style speed boat. (A Secret Service man actually hurt his back when he fell on the transom of the boat as the president accelerated with more g-force than Apollo 11 on takeoff.)

Then there is the current President Bush's dramatic landing on an aircraft carrier moving at 20 knots in the Pacific Ocean. (The Navy Viking jet in which he was riding snagged the fourth wire, the last wire on the carrier, just feet before the edge of the landing platform. In an ideal landing, a fighter jet would grab the third wire.) We watched the president climb down from the cockpit wearing a fighter pilot's high-altitude flight suit and carrying a Top Gun helmet. The image made Tom Cruise look like a Piper Cub pilot.

Bush's staged arrival was too Hollywood even for Hollywood and perhaps even for an unreconstructed, hell-bent-for-leather Texan like the current president.

The only image more inappropriate might be Secretary of State Colin Powell arriving in a jump jet. Nevertheless, as a former general and ex-head of the Joint Chiefs of Staff, Powell could at least legitimately say he missed being back in the day.

But in the present president's defense, he did learn how to fly a jet in the Texas Air National Guard. His critics would say, however, when he flew, he did so over Houston not Hanoi.

A second "but" – but both he and his father are/were pilots. Bush the elder was a World War II bomber pilot, who on his 75th birthday in 1999, decided to make a parachute jump just to see what it would be like to jump voluntarily from a plane. (Bush bailed out of a plane that was hit by anti-aircraft fire during World War II over Japan. He said, 54 years later, he just wanted to try parachuting when he didn't *have* to do it. More startling is the fact that he made the jump even though he wasn't running for anything.)

Then there is the photo op gone wrong for someone who wanted to be president. Will Mike Dukakis ever live down the photo of him wearing the Snoopy leather helmet with his head sticking out of the battle tank on maneuvers in Michigan? He really did look like a kid on a carousel. Cynics and wags might say he likes to ride and that could explain why he works the rails for Amtrak now. (Dukakis retorted, "Hey, I never threw up over the Japanese prime minister." Bush, the elder, did this in Tokyo in 1992.)

Nevertheless, the practice of image-making will not likely change, primarily because there were some photo ops that did work. Take, for example, President Reagan in 1987 in a speech at the Brandenburg Gate in West Berlin telling "Mr. Gorbachev, tear down this wall!" Then there is the enduring image of President Carter bringing together that famous three-person woven handshake of himself, Egypt's Anwar al-Sadat and Israel's Menachem Begin at the announcement of the Camp David Accords peace agreement in 1978.

In the frantic campaign days to come in 2004, we will witness more staged images to be sure. We should look at them with the perspective of the wary consumer and try to determine which ones are not real and which ones actually represent the person who represents us in Washington.

9.

SUPER BOWL XL:
MICK ENTERS THE STONE AGE

The very first thing I did after watching 62-year-old Mick Jagger waving his arms around during the Super Bowl Half Time Show was to run to my home gym and do triceps extensions until I felt the burn. In my case, the burn came after about 12 reps.

But, nevertheless, I felt better knowing that maybe I could forestall having upper arms that had zero muscle tone like Mick's. When he clapped his hands over his head to urge the crowd on, his arms looked like little jibs on a sailboat flapping in the wind. How can he have such flabby arms when he is so cadaverous?

Now granted, for his age, Jagger, overall, looks good and moves well. Nothing wrong with those swivel hips or that flat belly. But thank goodness the cameras were shooting from downtown Cleveland or the millions of TV watchers would have been treated to facial wheel ruts not seen since the silent movie days.

At the risk of making my fellow boomers angry, there probably is an age beyond which one should not dance on a stage while wearing an outfit that shows off parts of the body. The age varies with the individual, of course, but I sincerely hope Madonna doesn't decide to dance to "Material Girl" when she is 62.

It is true, however, that some people are ageless. Vanna White is still telegenic after decades of letter flipping on "The Wheel of Fortune." Dick Clark is a gerontological miracle. But for the most part, even with botox, plastic surgery and Hollywood makeup, most people cannot look 20 when they are three times 20.

It was refreshing to hear Aretha Franklin belt out the "Star Spangled Banner," proving that there are some things older performers can still do.

Come to think of it there are a number of things elderly people do perhaps without knowing:

They don't swivel their heads around when they are backing up in a car but instead rely on rearview and side mirrors.

They usually spot an elevator or an escalator long before a younger person does.

They don't throw Frisbees any longer.

They don't ride in tippy kayaks or canoes as much as they used to.

They seem to eat more dinners while sitting in their recliners than before.

They seem to be always turning on more lights.

They seem to forget to turn off other lights like directional signals which seem to stay on as long as their trips last.

They sit closer to the fire.

They sit farther away from the band.

They carry lawn chairs in the trunks of their cars.

They carry three pairs of reading glasses in their briefcases, purses or glove compartments.

They tell more stories about the past.

They tell fewer stories about the present.

They take more medications.

They take less medical advice.

And they spend more time making lists like this one than they used to.

Mick and the Stones can still rock the house but I wish he would remember the lines from the old song that state: "I can't dance, don't make me."

10.

HELP, I'M BEING HELD AGAINST MY WILL IN E-MAIL JAIL

Napoleon employed five full-time secretaries to help him draft communiqués; I have just myself and e-mail. Now, at the risk of my readers thinking: "Oh, my gosh, Costa has finally gone over the edge, he thinks he's Napoleon," let me say I think everyone should have some ways or some people to help manage e-mail.

E-mail was designed to speed message flow but in practice it has evolved into a syrupy mess that gums up mainframes and clogs personal computers.

E-mail manages me; I do not manage it. Every minute, several e-mail messages arrive. Some are spam, some are legitimate, all require action. I have tried virtually every method I know to try to bring order and maintain memory - mine and my computer's. They have failed.

First, I tried setting up subfolders into which I would put unread e-mails for sorting and processing.. This worked for about three hours. After having dragged and dropped 200 e-mails into 24 separate subfolders, I discovered that not only did I not know where anything was but that some messages were time-sensitive and I had missed key deadlines.

Then I tried opening each e-mail as it came in and doing whatever was necessary to make it final. Now, in the newspaper world, this can involve the following steps:

Open e-mail; read it; open attachment; highlight, copy and paste into a Word template; edit/rewrite the text for newspaper style, grammar and for anything that a libel lawyer would lick his/her chops over; highlight, cut and paste into network file for typesetting; open digital photo attachment; change dpi from National Geographic quality that requires a gigantic 14 megabytes to something that won't bog down our mainframe; copy to separate photo subfolder; then, finally, close-out message and move on to the next one.

This method works well but on an average day takes about two hours of uninterrupted time. Oh, and while I am doing the real-time editing of e-mails, another 70 non-spam e-mails arrive.

By the way, why do people slug every e-mail to me as a "press release?" The news would be if it were not a press release. So, when I try to search the subject line of an e-mail I have 596 messages that state: press release.

I have tried printing out hard copies of all e-mails that require action. This kills a lot of trees and hurts my retinas.

I have tried using Outlook's alleged tools to flag certain items or to write rules to handle messages in different ways. These methods didn't work either.

Many of my e-mail senders are angry that I do not usually have time to respond to them. Responding means opening, opening means time sink. So, I choose not to send out 223 responses a day.

So, as the combination boss-admin that I am, I find myself stuck in e-mail jail.

I get persistent error messages that command me to delete cubic tons of e-mails or my e-mails will not be able to be forwarded, replied to or moved. In addition to the automatic e-mail warnings that pop on my screen like the gas pump icons on my dashboard when I am low on gas, I also get personalized encouragement from our network administrator who urges me to move 798 e-mail messages to my hard drive or face electrocution.

So, I comply. I highlight screens and screens of messages and delete them, then empty them into dark matter space. But just as I do, battalions more march onto my screen.

Therefore, I appeal to you out there. Do you know how to get unstuck from e-mail molasses? Send me your solutions via pcosta@cnc.com. I'll even respond to them - or if I cannot seem to break away, I'll enlist one of Napoleon's secretaries and have him quill you a reply.

11.

WHAT DID YOU DO THIS HOLIDAY WEEKEND, ANYTHING FUN?

The long holiday weekend is over and now come the questions? "How was your weekend? Do anything fun?" "Hey, good morning, do anything interesting over the weekend?"

Well, after getting five of these questions just traversing the newsroom to my so-called workstation I am always tempted to inflate my real life experiences and say:

"Yeah, it was great. Went ocean kayaking on Saturday, hang gliding on some mean thermals in New Hampshire on Sunday, mountain biking on Monday and on Friday night went to the 23rd Annual Conference on Special Relativity at MIT."

When, actually, this Memorial Day weekend I mowed the lawn, glanced through some old Brookstone catalogues and watched "CSI" reruns.

Now, of course, when the sports guys ask me what I did I vary the big talk. After all, these guys curl what I bench press so I don't want to get caught in too great an exaggeration. "Just cooked some sirloin on the grill and listened to the White Sox - Angels game on satellite radio. You know, on paper and in the field, the White Sox are a better team but they just don't get the press the Cubs get. The Cubs have been Chicago's team since the mid-1990s and they get all the attention - much of it undeserved."

I'm hoping this bit of conversation will establish my regular-guy credentials in sportsland as I write about magical realism in the latest novel I am reviewing for the arts page.

I also have fantasies of writing the perfect résumé as well. I always wanted to write a couple of lines under hobbies and personal interests that would read something like this:

HOBBIES
Windsurfing, judo, chess, power lifting, madrigal singing, mountain climbing, woodworking, harpsichord playing and competitive skeet shooting.

Well, maybe I would not include the skeet shooting because a lot of employers are uneasy about employees who have familiarity with guns. Perhaps I would substitute something like rowing, eight-man crew. Rowing in eights is selfless torture and the ultimate in non-ego team play. I hear that's big in the corporate world - team play, that is, not non-ego team play.

Under skills I would include:

Fluent in Mandarin, ancient Greek, Excel, Unix, Linux, C++ and Assembler. And that would be if I were applying for a job in the non-technical world. For the technical world I would also include things like "experiment with surface-mount technology" and participate in math Olympiads under hobbies. I would also mention my participation in the Bach Society. I hear mathematicians love Bach.

But, you know, I think it is perfectly fine to spend time off not doing anything. My very favorite times are spent lying in a rope hammock in the shade looking at the green leaves fluttering in front of a blue sky with lazy cumulous clouds gliding by. That's cool and meaningful. I can play rugby some other weekend.

12.

WORKING WITH GRACE UNDER PRESSURE

Friday was bring-your-dog-to-work day so I did just that.

I put my daughter's 1-year-old, fawn-colored Pug, whose name is Grace, in her car harness, buckled her in and drove her to work. She slept most of the way, head on paws like a sphinx.

It was a quiet ride through leafy woods, around graceful s-turns that only New England and the Alps can offer.

The parking lot was only one-fourth full when we arrived. There was an unusual number of kayaks and canoes on top of car roofs. People were planning to escape from the gravity of work and glide on water during the soon-to-begin weekend.

We rode the elevator up and Grace was fascinated by the padded mover's blankets on the elevator walls. I thought, "if you think we need padded walls in the elevator, Grace, wait to you see the newsroom."

We walked down the long aisles of the newsroom past cubicles filled with old newspapers, dry faxes and empty cans of soda — all of which caused Grace to veer from her course as she, canine archaeologist, sniffed each pile of history.

Things were relatively quiet. The police and fire scanner would erupt from time to time and Grace would lift her head as she heard the signature sound of the squelch-tail at the end of each police transmission. (You know the sound when you hear it but it is difficult to describe. Just listen to the television program, "CSI," when Gus and Katherine arrive at the crime scene and you will hear dozens of squelch-tails in the background.)

My colleagues were sitting in front of their computer screens, typing away. I wondered what Grace thought they were doing because I am told that, unlike cats, dogs cannot see what is on a TV-like monitor. Perhaps Grace thought they were trying to stamp on ants with their fingers the way she does with her paws on sidewalks.

From time to time, humans would come over to meet Grace and they all talked in that very high voice big people use when they talk to small things. Grace would tilt her head to dial in the high frequencies of the women's voices, and occasionally, lie on the floor, paws apart, head up like a lioness on the prowl. She was ready to play chase but no one wanted to play.

After a while, she settled down and sat at my feet as I too began to stamp ants. Luckily for Grace, it was not a production deadline day in which people typically yell into telephones, slam down phonebooks, drop papers on the floor, or hum or mumble to themselves. Today was a planning and interviewing day and most of the reporters were out on their beats gathering news for the next editions of the papers.

Soon the confines of the cubicle seemed to be affecting even toy dog Grace, who weighs in at a mighty 17 pounds and stands about one and a half hands high. She wanted to get out there and romp.

Her boredom was relieved finally when a colleague of mine brought in his two, extremely well-behaved bigger dogs. One was an elegant golden retriever who looked down at Grace the way I presume King Henry VIII looked down from his throne at a court jester.

The other canine was a beagle/spaniel dog who was off-leash, and amazingly, obeyed voice commands. Grace responds to two voice commands: "sit" and "outside." When she is free of her leash and out in open grass she runs in circles around us until she collapses panting. After her heart recycles, she runs around once again like an electron around a nucleus.

After much sniffing and Grace's insistence at playfully nipping the beagle's ear, Grace followed me out of the newsroom to the parking lot where my wife was waiting to drive Grace back home.

I don't know what I learned from this take-your-dog-to-work experience except that the clichés are all true: dogs reflect their owners' personalities, little dogs are feisty, and absolutely no living creature can stay in a cubicle for long.

13.

MY WORD(S), WHAT'S A GLOVE BOX?

Words should have specific meanings.

Take "glove box." That's the rectangular door device built into your vehicle's dashboard. (What's a dashboard? We'll get to that later.) Well, a glove box is where drivers in their touring automobiles stored their leather gloves circa 1916. They wore gloves to help fight the friction from turning those giant, non-power steering wheels. The wheels on those early horseless carriages were huge like those seen on turn-of-the-century schooners. You can still see ships' wheels in old sea movies. They appear just before that inevitable time in the movie when the main character says: "Take the helm, I'm going below." Just after saying that, a gust of wind blows ocean spray against the sailor in the slicker who is working the wheel.

Back to the glove box. I looked inside mine recently and found no gloves. I did find a cheap 89-cent, red plastic flashlight whose D-cell batteries had fused into paste a year after Nixon resigned. (No connection between the two events.) Also inside, was a box of wet wipes that had dried out; a dozen or so pink receipts from the fast lube change outlet I go to (I noticed that they were the color of transmission fluid, a bad omen); a pencil-type tire pressure gauge so old that its scale maximum was a pre-SUV 36 pounds of pressure and an old comb.

Still, no gloves. Our culture has left the glove box behind along with fedoras for men, pill box hats for women and bias-ply balloon tires with wide whitewalls.

It used to be that words like "glove box" or "ice box" meant just that — a place where gloves are stored, a box containing ice. Now previously precise words have been muddied, mangled, mixed up, and sometimes even murdered.

"Dial-up service." That actually means that your personal computer uses devices — a regular telephone line and a modem — to connect to the Internet or the World Wide Web. But there is no dial; it's done with "touch tones." Wait a minute. What touch? No fingers do the walking here. The computer automatically emits a sequence of tones over the phone lines to another computer that recognizes the tones and does certain things with that tone package — like disconnect you the second after you connect.

The dial-up phrase is illogical. But I admit I am the same "logical" guy who went out to an expensive restaurant recently to discuss how to control the family budget.

I used to blame all things video for the devaluation of the word. I realize, however, that this may not be the case. More people listen to words than ever before these days over digital music devices like iPods, portable CD players and cell phones. There is even a very popular genre of word-songs: rap. And yet, sharply defined words are fading from the lexicon. We have new multi-purpose words like "impact," which can be a verb, a noun or a movie title.

It bothers me more than most because I allegedly work in the profession of the printed word. Ink on paper. We are supposed to have a knowledge of proper usage, denotative and connotative meanings, idioms, slang, vogue words, spoonerisms and malapropisms. Sometimes, intentionally, we will splice words together like recombinant verbal DNA surgeons to try to be clever and cut into the reader's consciousness. Other times, we merely meld ancient but active English words like "chortle" into our prose. Chortle is one of those verbs often used in fables and nursery rhymes but almost never experienced outside the world of the printed word. The wolf in the "Three Little Pigs" was the kind of villain who would chortle after hearing of someone's misfortune.

But I am not claiming there are no active or precise words and phrases today. For example, take "juice box." Now there is a new phrase to describe what kids drink for lunch. It also complies with the "ice box" precision rule. I also like the less-precise but descriptive expression of someone who goes "postal."

In closing, as promised, here is the 411 on the word "dashboard." According to Merriam Webster's Third New International Dictionary (unabridged version), dashboard means "a screen of wood or leather placed on the forepart of a horse-drawn carriage, sleigh, or other vehicle to intercept water, mud, or snow thrown up by the heels of the horses."

By the way, as we all know, car dashboards have dials in them. Maybe they should be called dial-up dashboards.

14.

TROLLING FOR A FISHING LICENSE

I went to town hall the other day to buy an annual resident fishing license.

I buy one every year and pin it to my fishing vest. The license seems to function as a warning to fish that the wearer is absolutely no danger to anything aquatic. I swear the fish must be able to read because as I troll by the shores every year with all kinds of gurgling, psychedelic lures, I manage to snag only wayward weeds. A morning without a weed is a great fishing day for me.

Anyway, the good town clerk greeted me as she stood behind the high counter (I wonder why the counters are so high? Is there gold back there? Do they think we fishermen will vault over the counter and steal the gold?) After exchanging pleasantries, I told her I would like to buy a fishing license. No can do, she said. "We don't sell them anymore. You have to get them at the outdoor store in the next town over." That's all she said. What outdoor store? Do I call 411 and say: "Get me the outdoor store, pronto."

Nobody knows where the elusive outdoor store is. I asked around at several gas stations. "Isn't it somewhere in Acton?" one guy said. Another thought there may be one in Cambridge. Another guy said, "There's definitely one in Lee."

Lee? I said I needed a Massachusetts license not a New York one.

Look, I only want a simple fishing license. You know, the kind on which you lie about your height and weight. Amazingly each year as I get older I grow slightly taller and lighter. I figure by the time I retire I'll be as thin as Fred Astaire. Can you imagine him trying to sit still in a boat for three hours? "Fred, stop dancing around, you're scaring the fish."

I went to the fishing department at a national retail chain. I hefted a nice graphite rod and caught a salesman, or rather, he caught me. "It's a beauty isn't it? With the right line you can cast about 100 yards with it," he said. "Great. Hey, do you know where I can buy a fishing license?" I asked.

"You can't." he said.

"I can't?"

"No, have to buy them online now," he said and took the rod from me and placed it back in the display rack, disappointed not to land a sale but just field a question.

Online, eh? Of course, everything is online now, why not licenses. Although how will they know if I am as slender as I say I am? At the clerk's office, the clerk could look applicants over and say, "Hey, guy, no way are you 175 pounds and 6' 2. Who do you think you are, Ted Williams in his prime?"

Why does the state have to know my dimensions anyway? It is not as if I would use my fishing license to board an airplane or sneak into Canada - although I hear the fishing is extremely good in Canada. And the only assault I make on a lake is that I drag a thin mono-filament line through the water for three hours and go home. I figure I use up seven drops of lake water that fall into the boat and evaporate. Not much of an environmental impact.

So, after going through the dot-gov maze online, I found the right site. After giving them my latest credit card number, the only one left that is not maxed out, I signed off knowing that my license will be winging its way to my mailbox soon. I expect it about the time the geese have called it a season and are honking back south. I'll get maybe four days of fishing in. Not bad for nearly $30.

At least I didn't have to drive to the outdoor store in Lee.

15.

My PC is a Fatal Error

It has been a challenging week here at the Westford Eagle. We mustered our forces, and with the help of local historians and friends in the community, put together a 32-page supplement celebrating Westford's 275th Anniversary.

This effort put our technology to the test and, of course, it failed. Our server ground to a halt last night. It had decided enough was enough. Luckily for those of us on deadline, the server was revived about an hour later. The server meltdown was the last in a series of technology events this week.

Earlier, a laptop computer I sometimes use to write this very column sent me a persistent error message: "... missing operating system." That was it, three little words (all lowercase). It also seemed to take the time to include the ellipsis. You would think if it could do that, why not find the missing system? I was almost tempted to ask around the newsroom: "Hey, any of you see my operating system? Did I leave it in the lunchroom?"

But I am told missing means something else in the digital world. I asked one of my computer-savvy colleagues to look at the problem for me. She did everything she could to try to resurrect the missing system. She surfed the Internet and asked questions on user boards about the problem. She downloaded an executable program to try to jumpstart the system. She went into the OZ-land of MS-DOS and did non-mouse-generated commands using symbols and techniques not seen since Wozniak worked on the first Apple in his garage.

At one point I wanted to suggest spraying the hard drive with WD-40 or giving the carburetor a good dose of Gumout®. I did not go so far as to suggest we apply pig fat to the axle holding the wagon wheels. My contemporary helper would not appreciate those suggestions to be sure. She was used to wireless interfaces and I was still looking to see where I could change the ribbon on the printer. They don't have ribbons, I discovered to my typewriter-nostalgic dismay. They use ink cartridges.

Eventually after hours of partitioning the hard disk, allocating sectors, reloading and reconfigurating, she came to the conclusion that the had drive was "fried." Hopeless. Officer down. Send SWAT.

I think someone should write a mystery novel based on computer error messages. I always get the ones that are terminal. "Fatal error." Other users get messages that say "Hit any key to continue;" I get the ones that say hit any key and you will lose all your data, lock up the machine and blow a fuse in your house's commercial AC supply.

Also, when other people lose or misplace a file in Word, they go into the "find" menu and type in a few letters, and voila, there is their missing file. I go into the find function and type in what I am looking for and before my finger even leaves the return key I get the message: "0 files found." I want to say what my mother would ask me when I couldn't find my school notebook: "Did you even look?"

My luck with computer printers rivals my CPU prowess. Why is it that the most difficult thing to do in the computer world is stop and purge a print job. I have tried everything but it seems once I send those bits and bytes down the line to the printer they are like salmon in heat. They will jump up roaring waterfalls and leap huge arcs into the air on their way up the digital version of the Columbia River.

All I get are blinking amber lights. Think of them as hazard lights on the printer. I press the buttons, go into deep menus only seen by the technicians who helped Nebuchadnezzar build his temple, and still the directory informs me that there are 74 print jobs in queue waiting to be printed.

So, I have no remedy but to bring the laptop to one of those national computer franchises where they charge $180 for you just to slide the laptop across the counter to them. No, they don't need the power supply or mouse. Why not? Make me feel good and say you need the supply and mouse because: "You are right, Mr. Customer, you know your machine." Actually, they think: "How did this guy manage to work the automatic door to get in here in the first place? What an incredible Luddite."

Putting in a new hard drive, reconfiguring the disk, reinstalling the software and leading the missing operating system back home by the ear, will all cost me just $175 less than the entire cost of a new machine or about $1,400.

It has been a tough week at the paper indeed.

16.

FALL: WET LEAVES, CLANGING FURNACES AND SIDEWALK SAND

After weeks of record rain, I am now ready for a wicked winter.

In a season of abnormalities — like hurricanes so numerous they make it all the way through the alphabet — it is comforting to know that a few things are familiar and "normal" this time of year. The Red Sox, as is the usual case, are not headed for the World Series, the New England Patriots have lost half their games so far, and the dull, monochromatic fall foliage looks like something you might see on the rim of the Mojave Desert.

Scientists say the polar ice caps are melting at an alarming rate and this will have consequences on our climate. I always seem to get their predictions mixed up. Does global warming mean there will be more precipitation and therefore more snow or does it mean there will just be more rain? Are those coyotes we are seeing in our back yards or are they really wooly mammoths?

I'm told tanning salons are experiencing one of their best fall seasons ever. I have to ask people in the alphabet (X,Y and Z) generations about this. The last time people my age got a dose of ultraviolet radiation was when the U.S. military was doing nuclear testing in the atmosphere.

Another fall event is the onslaught of wet leaves that clog street drains, collect around corners on country roads and make the streets slicker than Teflon. These troublesome objects have also amassed in eaves troughs and sit there in a mucky mess daring us to risk life and limb as we ascend our ladders. As you know, this is the time in my home maintenance cycle when I don my climber's rappelling gear and hang from the chimney on the roof as my neighbors watch from their porches, cell phones in hand, ready to dial 911.

I even have a car old enough to require the fall ritual of installing snow tires. My car is one of those rear-wheel-drive bombs that draws thumbs up from teenagers when they come astride it at a traffic light. I bought some new snow tires for it last weekend and was the only one in the waiting room. I watched as the tire guys gathered around the car remarking how they had friends who had similar souped-up models. Not too comforting to know that the 19-year-old car I am driving is not a restored classic but an actual, drive-to-work vehicle. Haven't I heard of metal fatigue? How about planned obsolescence?

My fireplace is a wreck. I forgot that I had burned boxes of old canceled checks, financial statements and other written documents you wouldn't want your neighbors to read. Their charred remains huddle in the fireplace like black and brittle goblins. I will need to shovel those into a trash bag without getting any on the living room rug. This means I have to lay out last Sunday's paper like a paper version of the ramp of an amphibious landing craft at D-Day. Even though I will take these elaborate precautions my CSI spouse will detect smudges and carbon traces abundant enough to get me indicted on two counts of sloppy fall maintenance.

My furnace guy keeps calling me. He would like to come over and clean out the furnace for the upcoming heating season. This has become a more than $100 ritual and I am beginning to wonder how clean a furnace needs to be to burn at only 72 percent efficiency anyway.

It is also time to mow the lawn that one last time and put the cover on the air conditioner. I have already tried to buy some sand for the upcoming ice season but my home supply store says I am rushing things. Maybe I am. I remember my experience on my fieldstone slate stairs a few years ago. I was walking down the stairs carrying an antique cathedral style radio to take to a swap meet when I slipped on the ice. The radio launched into an arc like the opening scene in the space odyssey film "2001" when the apes throw a bone into the air. I landed at the base of the stairs like a beginning gymnast on the parallel bars. I definitely didn't "stick" the landing.

This year I am determined to sand the stairs at the slightest hint of freezing temperatures. I'll just keep my shop vacuum at the ready. After all, sand in the living room is normal; it's fall.

17.

DRY-GULCHED AT THE DRY CLEANERS

It is Saturday morning at 8. I have 20 minutes to make it to the dry cleaners before the line starts to form.

In particular I want to avoid the guy who comes every Saturday morning to pick up his 14 shirts on hangers. Every week, 14 shirts. Now my theory is the guy works in the corporate world during the day and is a maitre d' at a posh seafood restaurant at night. Why else would he need 14 shirts when we regular guys only need five?

He pays his bill with a credit card and then bear hugs his shirts and walks out the door. You can hear a rustle of plastic as he squeezes through the door jam.

If I can avoid him, then the only other guys I have to look out for are the inevitable two guys who pick up Persian rugs that have just been cleaned. Now these rugs are usually 12 feet by 9 feet and weigh about as much as the full sarcophagus of Tutankhamen. No problem for these guys who sport deltoid muscles as big as soccer balls. They each grab an end and somehow manage to twist and turn just enough to get the rug out the door and into their white van. The vans are always white. Why is that?

Then there is the lady who does a complete 12-minute download about all her children's activities to the woman behind the counter. I don't have the emotional bandwidth on a Saturday morning for this, but endure it I must or lose my place in line.

Then it is my turn. I present my ticket and the woman presses a button and the conga line of clothes moves a few feet and stops. She takes out a plastic bag and places it on the hanging bar next to the cash register. She tears off the bill and places it on the counter. I look at it as it rests upside down. I take out my wallet and count out $32.50. The cashier looks at me quizzically.

"That's $132.50, sir," she says with a smile.

"One hundred-thirty-two fifty?" I gasp. Can't be, I think. That's more than I paid as a down payment on my daughter's 1990 Dodge Neon.

"Why so much?" I inquire, reaching for my credit card.

"Well, sir, there are two men's suits, three pairs of men's slacks, four silk blouses, two women's skirts, four scarves, a woman's sweater and three women's pantsuits. That's a lot of cleaning," she said and broke into the smile of a hang 'em judge.

I am trapped. I can't say, "Hey, take the clothes back, I don't want them." I have got to ransom them somehow, even if this means going into credit card debt at 29 percent interest on a very large unpaid balance.

I am convinced that Generations X, Y, Z folks do not use dry cleaners for their clothes but find some other way to clean them. Gallons of Woolite?

The only thing more expensive than the local dry cleaners is having one's clothes cleaned and pressed at a four-star hotel. There it is $50 for a man's suit.

I look at the two suits of mine that were dry cleaned. One I bought from an outlet store in Maine, the other from a discount store in lower Manhattan, six years ago. The lapel widths are suspiciously wide — not as wide as the ones worn by vaudeville comedians circa 1921, but wider than Mr. Armani ever used on any of his suits. (I have never owned an Armani suit, by the way, but I have coveted them whenever I see them advertised in a glossy men's magazine.)

I take the clothes off the rack and walk slowly to my car.

The only thing dry about this cleaners is that it drained my wallet of any liquidity at all. Well, I don't care. Maybe I'll take the family out to the sea food restaurant tonight and see whether Mr. 14 shirts will give me a good table with a water view.

18.

LET THEM EAT CAKE AND DONUTS

Hello, my name is Peter and I am addicted to sugar.

But the only 12-step program I am on is the one in which I try to avoid eating the 12 donuts in the Dunkin' Donuts box in one sitting.

I crave the cane. From my 6 a.m. cup of coffee with enough sugar to sweeten the Missouri River, to my midnight snack of frosted wheat, I ingest enough of the sweet substance to send a platoon of pit bulls into diabetic coma.

My problem is DNA-deep, I am sure, and one which was made worse by growing up in the kitchen of a professional baker. My mother made wedding cakes, birthday cakes, and pastries of all kinds. It was not unusual for me as a child to have cake for breakfast with a glass of chocolate milk. My dentist was dismayed at the risk I was placing on the enamel of my teeth and my synapses snapped with enough voltage to make Ritalin nervous. (The calming drug had not been developed in my day. I soared through adolescence bouncing off the walls of the cafeteria. How pathetic is it that my student work job in the cafeteria was to sell ice cream?)

I was the new boy in second grade who brought in a birthday "train" cake, complete with steam engine and coal car, made by my mother. The train cake sported Oreo Cookie wheels, 2 Hershey's chocolate bars in the shape of a V for a cow catcher and a smoke stack of dark European chocolate - all accessories to the cake body of the train, which also was made of chocolate with thick frosting. Needless to say, I was a very popular and a very jittery boy in second grade.

As I grew older, I enjoyed baklava breakfasts followed by honey cake lunches, ending with TV snacks of brownies the size of continents topped with Himalayas of Cool Whip®. When I would visit my friends' houses as a boy, I was always surprised that there was only one kind of dessert per meal being served. Usually, they were something as dry as chalk like English scones or boringly bland like vanilla cookies.

Where were the four-layer cakes, the strawberry tortes, the chocolate mouse? They were at my mother's in-house bakery. That's where.

(An aside: My mother wrote a letter to the Peter Paul Mounds Company years ago and said she had two boys, Peter and Paul, who loved Mounds candy bars. Well, the good people at Mounds sent along a complimentary case of Mounds. I think there were 144 bars. They lasted three weeks.)

To this day, I can't stand being sugar-shy. I find I write my best headlines after eating a chocolate glazed donut. Two donuts by 9 a.m. and I think I am writing headlines so clever George Bernard Shaw would be speechless.

My boss says she can set her watch by my afternoon run to the candy machine. I usually arrive at the machine like a blue jay at the feeder by 2:34 p.m., give or take 15 seconds.

I have tried when I have been on diets to reduce my sugar intake. I can eliminate the desserts for a few months, but I cannot drink coffee without sugar or down a soft drink sweetened with chemicals. How do all those super models drink gallons of soda laced with artificial sweeteners? The after-taste causes rumbles in my stomach that last longer than a PGA golf match. Maybe that's why the models are so thin. They must have constant stomach aches.

One would think that I would have systemic troubles from the grotesque amounts of sugar I abuse my body with, but my blood sugar level is actually on the low side. (OK, you armchair physicians, don't send me a flood of e-mails telling me that's why I eat so much sugar in the first place. Hypoglycemia you say?)

What to do, what to do? My New Year's Day-type resolutions don't work but I know I need to lessen the amount of sugar I eat. Yet, just thinking of losing all that sweetness turns me sour.

I think I'll double back to the candy machine while my boss is busy checking my pages.

19.

'DOWN TALKERS' CAN REALLY RUIN YOUR DAY

Comedian Jerry Seinfeld coined the word, "close talker," to describe those people who stand too close to you when speaking. The present bad economic times have generated a new personality type, which to bowdlerize Seinfeld, we can call the "down talker." Down talking is the reverse of one-upmanship.

An example. Just the other day I heard someone say that a friend of his was still out of work even after 13 months of aggressive job seeking. The person to whom he was speaking, resorted to down talking: "You think that's bad? My cousin's dad in Michigan has been unemployed since the layoffs following the closing of the DeSoto auto plant in 1957."

Nothing ever seems bad enough without someone feeling the need to descend one step down the depression staircase. This also happens in social situations. Another overheard conversation: "I have known him for about a month now and we still haven't been out on an official date." Down talker: "Big deal. I haven't been asked out on an official date since the seventh grade."

Down talking is particularly common among older people who say things like: "When I was your age, we didn't even have anything but radio for news and entertainment, never mind all this digital stuff that kids carry around with them."

The other day I was talking to someone from Generation X or Y (I'm never sure which one because my boomer generation is so old it predates the alphabet generations) and I actually said: "When I was your age, I was a jerk. In fact, most people are jerks until they are about 35." I'm awfully glad I admitted that about myself and about those in my age cohort because it is true. During our twenties and thirties, we are consumed by trying to establish ourselves and our careers - in many cases trying to find any career, never mind one that fits us or is a true "calling."

Also we are starting to form personal relationships and trying to find a place to live of our own like a real adult, etc. These quests take lots of energy and time and deplete whatever store of kindness we have and we often behave badly during those establishing decades.

There may also be some time-released substance coiled in the double helix of our DNA that mysteriously enters our system at age 35 and gets us to slow down, look around and realize that there are others besides ourselves with the same or greater problems and challenges. So, until then, we act like jerks.

So today, couple the X, or should we call it the Y-Me?, generation's angst with down talking and you have a pretty gloomy garden to walk through indeed.

But I don't see "up talking" as a solution. Can you imagine telling a friend about some problem and having him or her say: "Well, yes, but you're working, healthy and young and tomorrow a cold front is coming that will break the heat wave and the Red Sox can still win a wild card spot." (Maybe they could have a victory parade with the players riding in DeSoto convertibles.)

People like to commiserate and complain. That will always be true — especially if they are under 35 and tend to display the inner child/jerk. Now, of course, there are exceptions to the under-35 rule, and you run into people who are genuinely nice all the time. We call them: mothers.

20.

GAMUT, GAUNTLET, MADONNA, STING

I don't know Madonna's last name. But then I don't know either of Sting's names. I know Prince was formerly known as The Artist just as I know that Frank Sinatra was called The Chairman of the Board. The Duke was Duke Ellington and the Count was Count Basie - easy to remember those jazz legends because of their first names. But, of course, lording it over all of these performers is Elvis, who has become known simply as The King.

But most people these days do not really care about names or words or the etymology of same. I heard someone the other day in the newsroom say that he had "jerry-rigged" his computer. Well, he meant jury-rigged, of course, which means makeshift rigging. Jury-rigging was something you did when you snapped a mast in a heavy sea off Pitcairn Island.

People have become foggy about words, probably because they are exposed to so few of them now with the explosion of all things video. It is as if - and I will use a film reference here just to show that I can - people today were extras in the film in which the Voyager probe was found by beings in another solar system. Dust had covered a portion of the probe's name and the other-worldly beings called the probe, Vger, and pronounced it vee-jer, instead of Voyager.

Many people today are using words that resemble original words but with dust on them. Someone recently said they had a variety of items, so many, that they ran the whole "gauntlet." What they meant to say was "gamut," as in the whole range. I would much rather be involved with things that run the gamut from soup to nuts than running any gauntlet, which is just plain nuts.

We all make mistakes and mishear words over the years. Until two years ago when a friend pointed out my mistake to me, I used to say "Antartica." He asked why I dropped the first "c" in the word because Antarctica is the antipode of the Arctic and the Arctic has a "c" in it. (I try to remember it now as "c" for cold.)

Language changes and should change through nuances of usage but not because of dusty minds. There is a richness to our language made lively and vital when we use just the right word in our speech or writing. And, yes, I recognize that spoken language is looser, more colloquial and idiomatic than written speech but both can be brightened by selecting the apposite word. (I don't think more than 10 people who are not octogenarians, have used the word, apposite, since 1925. I guess I should have used the more modern-sounding word, appropriate, instead.)

Whatever, you say? Now, as someone who loves the interplay of words, I find the use of whatever to be a verbal putdown. It means: I don't care whatever you just said or whatever you think. Let's hope that word remains relegated to the verbal arsenal of pre-teens.

So, let's try to rekindle the verbal fires and use the correct word and expression. We owe it to the brain cells we still have left.

By the way, Sting's birth name is Gordon Mathew Sumner. Madonna, as many may not know, was born Louise Veronica Ciccone. That's right, her real name is Louise. Somehow I have trouble calling the Material Girl Louise. She would undoubtedly retort: whatever. And I am sure I wouldn't be able to resist looking hurt and saying to her: jeez, Louise.

21.

GOOGLE EAVESDROPPING:
SEARCH OR SEARCH AND SEIZURE

Now, any NSA language specialist checking this string of searches might jump to the conclusion that something afoul is afoot.

The Justice Department has sued the search engine company, Google, and has demanded one week's worth of Web searches and one million addresses from the company's database.

Now this is troubling news for those of us who use Google every five minutes and for those of us who wish to protect our rights to privacy. The danger of having someone in a basement at the NSA examining our Web searches and concluding that we are bad guys is enormous. (Normally I would Google "NSA" to make sure that it is located in Washington and not in Langley, Virginia along with the CIA, but I am already on enough NSA lists, thank you very much.)

Let's look at some of my recent Google searches. I often use Google to check on spellings or to refresh my memory on items I refer to in this column. Here are some recent Internet searches I made in writing my CostaLiving columns:

uranium-238
plutonium
half-life
radioactive cleanup

Now, any NSA language specialist checking this string of searches might jump to the conclusion that something afoul is afoot. I wasn't interested in making a bomb but actually was just writing about the Patriots losing their playoff game to Denver. Furthermore, I was reminiscing about the 16 - 7 loss of the Baltimore Colts to the New York Jets in the Super Bowl III (Jan. 12, 1969) that generated sadness that had a half life longer than uranium-238. I was also going to write that mental health workers had a bigger job than hazmat handlers during a radioactive cleanup.

By the way, I would also go to Google to look up the words "afoul" and "afoot." I like the way those two words look in type and also like the fact that these two words were so often used by Elizabethan playwrights. So I am doing my bid to keep Shakespeare alive (or was it really Christopher Marlowe?) Yes, I used Google to make sure it was Marlowe who some people think really wrote all the plays attributed to Shakespeare. I remain firmly in the bard's camp. Marlowe, shmarlowe, I say.

Here is another string I used the Web to check on:
chador
Khomeini
Iranian hostage crisis
Col. Charles A. Beckwith

This string would certainly cause an NSA Iranian specialist to sit up straight. My interest here was to write a column about the 25th anniversary of the U.S. hostage crisis in Iran. The person in power in Iran at the time was the Ayatolla Khomeini and the man leading the failed 1980 rescue attempt in the dust storms of the Iranian desert was U.S. Army Col. Charles Beckwith. I was also going to mention metaphorically that the events inside the U.S. Embassy in Tehran at the time were as hidden from view as if they were covered with a chador. (It is a long, usually black, head-to-toe dress worn by traditional Iranian women and dates to the 6th century BC when Cyrus the Great was in power. All this information from Google, of course.)

Then there is this string:
George W. Bush language
nuclear
Bush twins
State of the Union

The word nuclear automatically sets off bells at Internet monitoring stations all over the NSA. Any inquiry into the commander in chief similarly is flagged. Also, why does this Web surfer want to know about members of the first family? The State of the Union speech shows the Google user may have political motives. In this case, however, I was just writing about funny language anomalies and how President Ford also could not say nuclear. Like Bush, Ford always pronounced it nuke-u-ler. But then, even three-time Pulitzer prize-winner Thomas Friedman of The New York Times used to say nuke-u-ler when he appeared on PBS' "Washington Week." (By the way, where is Tom now?) As for the Bush twins, I was just curious to know whether they had gotten jobs in the still-sluggish Bush economy.

That's all for now. I've got to do a MapQuest on the NSA. I didn't know it was in Fort Meade, Maryland. Thank goodness for Google.

22.

DIETING, DR. ATKINS AND PATTI HEARST

Dr. Atkins is ruining my life.

Heretofore, I was a happy, slightly overweight (my words) guy consuming gargantuan amounts of carbohydrates. Blissfully, I would spring from my recliner to the refrigerator in speeds that could challenge a cornerback in the National Football League. My run-silent-run-peanut butter night-time carb raids are legendary.

My excuses for eating badly were imaginative and inspired. I could convince Virginia Wolfe why I was eating this or that by citing some twice-told tale of nutritional folk lore. "This toast helps settle my stomach.," or "This rice helps absorb the stomach acids," that sort of thing. But then my brothers came under the influence of those carbo-counting fanatics loyal to the Atkins diet. They both had lost weight and were trimmer and possessed renewed energy. Their weight loss, they claimed, had changed their lives. They were happier, healthier, more energetic, more youthful-looking, even nicer guys because they were free from their carbohydrate addictions.

I listened to them exchanging recipes recently at a family gathering at a restaurant where I was the only one having dessert: a hot fudge sundae. (I managed to order one by using the ruse of sharing it with my niece and nephew.) The adults looked at me as if I were a member of the Gambino crime ring and was introducing children to cocaine. I immediately stopped eating the sundae and drank my mineral water.

What is it about people who lose weight and develop the dieter's equivalent of the Stockholm Syndrome? They become thin Patti Hearsts. All that is missing is the machine gun Patti held in that California bank. Do they do so to fight their own internal demons who constantly threaten to turn them back to streets paved with sugar? Or does a lack of carbohydrates make one slightly unbalanced?

To make matters worse, they use the dismissive lingo of the converted. "He's just craving carbs," they say to describe my lack of will power. Or, "He is protein-deficient and just can't see it."

Now, you should know that I admit to being a card-carrying, lifetime member of one of the nationally known weight loss programs. Every five years or so, I go back to the program and lose the 15 pounds I usually gain every five years. I am about to return soon. But, nevertheless, even when I was so slim people were afraid to ask about my weight loss for fear that I may have some dreadful disease, even then, I never sought converts or was as adamant as the carb-control cadre.

An aside. There was a story that our weight-loss lecturer shared with us that was funny. She told us that we all had passions for some food that was not good for us. For her, it was Oreo cookies. She said she could not drive home from the market without tearing open a bag of Oreos and eating one or two — sleeves. The mental image I have of two empty sleeves of cookies makes me smile to this day. Also, the number of cookies that represents demonstrates how bad our addictions can get.

Once I wrote a feature story in which I described a celebrity as being overweight. Two days later I received a letter (this was before e-mail) that excoriated me for falling prey to conventional wisdom and believing that some guy who put together an insurance weight chart in 1951 had the right to dictate what we should weigh. The letter was from a group then called, Fat Liberation. Their motto was: "What you weigh is right." Their viewpoint was that we pay too much attention to questionable standards that should not apply to all people.

At the time, I thought the Fat Liberationists were wrong and that being obese is proven to be unhealthy and can be shown to shorten one's life. Being grossly overweight can also limit the quality of one's life as well. I still believe that one should care about one's weight and try to control it to maintain one's health. I don't think we have to be runway model thin, however.

At the same time, I think we need to ease up on militant diet-bombing propaganda. There are many ways to maintain moderation in one's diet and to stay healthy. There is no single Holy Grail of dieting.

I have to close now. I need to get a Coca-Cola® and some crackers. They settle my stomach.

23.

ON CV JOINT REPAIR AND
SURVIVING AUTO REPAIR WAITING ROOMS

Eventually you will need a CV joint in your vehicle. CV joints are technically known as constant velocity joints and are usually found on front-wheel drive vehicles. They are designed to have a half-life that matches exactly the warranty of your car. If you have a 6-year, 60,000-mile warranty, then your CV joint will die at 60,001. If you are unlucky and have a 12-month, 12,000-mile warranty, then your CV joint will need replacing at 12,001.

It's demonic. And the cost to replace a worn-out joint will be a combination of these three numbers: 486. If you drive a small compact car, then the CV will cost $486. A mid-size sedan will cost $684. An Alaska-sized SUV will cost $864. Uncanny, how three numbers serve all, isn't it?

The CV joint is as close to an automotive Ponzi scheme as you can get. Dealers and mechanics pyramid their services. One owner tells another owner who tells another, and sure enough, waiting rooms across America are filled with people sitting on plastic cafeteria-style chairs as their cars are being fixed. We try not to drink the waiting room's bitter 10-hour-old coffee with the chalky non-dairy sweetener. But after 47 minutes watching a tennis match on ESPN between two players known only to people south of 0 degrees latitude, we end up drinking the coffee.

We read the promotional material on the walls in the waiting room three times. It's amazing how fascinating this material can be after an hour. For example, little did we know how important it is to flush one's hydraulic brake system. The information states the consequences of dirty brake fluid with such starkness that we can envision ourselves plowing through a toll booth at 65 miles per hour as our foot is jammed against the brake pedal, which somehow has managed to feel exactly like stepping on a wet sponge.

And how about those shock absorbers? When they are worn out, not only do you risk suffering excessive tire wear and a bumpy ride, but the probability of rolling your vehicle over after leaving the parking lot on two wheels following a tiff with your boss increases dramatically.

The waiting room literature is filled with procedures you didn't know you needed. Ignore the 4-color glossy warnings and you most certainly face catastrophe. For example, it is crucial to drain and fill the transfer case. What's with this "transfer" thing, my car wants out? Well, it seems the transfer case is somehow connected rather vitally to the drive train of your vehicle and if you let its life's fluid grow dark then you risk needing a $6,234 transfer case replacement. Transmissions and transfer cases occupy a different spot on the periodic chart of car elements and reside among the heavy metals. Replacing them always requires four digits.

So, here are a few rules of thumb about car repair:

1. Don't read anything in the waiting room;

2. Never agree with the service manager that "while we have it up on the lift, we might as well replace the exhaust system, the struts, the shocks, the rotors, the transfer case, the brake lines and the anti-sway bar."

3. Bring a checkbook and not a credit card to the service area.

4. Think twice about spending more on a repair than the Blue Book value of your vehicle.

5. Learn to love tennis on television.

24.

THE TALE OF TWO COUCHES

Into everyone's life a couch must fall. Make that two couches in my life.

For 40 years, these two identical sofas in my mother-in-law's house sat facing each other like supertankers at a dock in Bahrain. Kids jumped on them, dogs napped on them and adults slept on them.

They were covered with a wool pattern of beige hues. Between these six-foot-long sofas was a large round coffee table made of oak, standing on four fluted columns that could just as easily have supported the roof of the Parthenon.

The coffee table's top had one detectable large round ring, archaeological evidence that it had once served to support a large potted plant. So the two couches served as parallel lines to the coffee table circle and there was some ancient, geometric harmony to the arrangement.

The couches had been covered three times in their 40-year history and the master upholsterer who had done the work had retired a decade ago. He was an old-fashioned craftsman who would come to the house and pick up the couches in his truck and bring them to his shop for refitting. He would also pick up various pillows and armchairs. His work was expensive but it was excellent. You could not detect a seam or stitch when he was done and his upholstery tack work could draw the admiration of silversmiths in Spain.

The couches were solid pieces of furniture constructed on a sturdy hardwood frame. They retained their angular shape and looked substantial, much more than functional. They appeared almost regal as they stood used but unbowed.

But the pillows had lost the last of their strength and now were pancakes. The fabric at the base of the couches was torn from too many bumps from kids' tricycles and Big-Wheel encounters.

There was a sociology of these couches as well. Here is where I sat and talked to my future mother-in-law, who was an English teacher, about books and the intriguing fluctuations and idiosyncrasies of the English language. My future father-in-law and I would leave the TV room during halftime of the Patriots' game and eat a snack while sitting on the couches. Here also is where my daughter took a nap with Miss Piggy and where Della the Labrador dog slept under the coffee table like some modern-day guardian of the temple. In those pre-digital days, Della would scratch her neck with a paw and the resulting tones were loud enough to change the channel on the TV. We were one of the few families to have a dog-activated remote.

    A family meeting was held last week and it was decided the couches had to go and in their places other period furniture that was still presentable would be placed.

    As the last man standing, the job of getting rid of the couches fell to me. I had help sliding them into my pickup truck and tied them down with two hefty ratchet straps. They looked odd in the bright sunlight, tipped on their sides as if they were taking their own much-needed naps. I drove them out to our town's transfer station/dump and backed them up to two cavernous dumpsters. After five minutes of struggling to remove the overly tight ratchet straps, I was able to slide the couches slightly toward the tailgate.

    Two men who had been unloading scrap wood from their own pickup truck, without conferring with each other, stopped their unloading and asked if I needed a hand. "Boy, do I," I said. One of them helped me lift one of the couches out and raise it over the edge of the dumpster. In one swift motion, we launched it into the bin. "Kabloom," the man said as it hit the bottom of the dumpster like a depth charge in the classic submarine movie, "Run Silent, Run Deep." The man joined his buddy and they carried the second couch over to the second bin and launched it on its way to the couch graveyard.

    "All right," the other man said. I thanked them and they said, "No problem, sir."

    I got in the truck and started to drive away. I cast a glance in the rearview mirror and saw the tops of the two hulks pointing up in the air - two wrecks that had sailed their last voyage.

    It will take all the force the compactor can muster to break those two, I thought. How appropriate a last thought for those couches. They really don't make them like that any longer. How grateful we are to have had their support.

25.

FLUENT IN THE SHOP TALK OF PUBLIC SAFETY

A long time ago early in my reporting career, I spent some time covering the New York City police department.

I rode around Manhattan in a patrol car with officers on call and I also helped cover the Son of Sam murders, which resulted in the subsequent capture of serial killer, David Berkowitz. He was initially called the .44 caliber killer during his rampage because he used a .44 caliber handgun to kill his victims. Later, when Berkowitz was captured and said he heard voices from his imagined monster-father "Sam" telling him to kill women he thought were acting like prostitutes, Berkowitz became forever known as the Son of Sam.

As a writer, I especially enjoyed the cop talk. I always presumed they spoke in quick shorthand because they spent their lives sensing out danger and had to be able to identify something or someone quickly and succinctly. A dead body was a "db," a victim was a "vic," a child molester was a "short eyes." People who committed suicide by jumping off a bridge were said to "commit water." Someone who jumped to his death from a tall building was said to "commit sidewalk." A police officer who had burned out and ended his own life by shooting himself with his service revolver - and, unfortunately there were a few each year who did so - was said to have "eaten his gun."

"Too bad about Collins. He ate his gun last night."

When detectives thought the evidence led to a particular suspect they had nicknamed, "Elvis," they said they "liked" Elvis for the crime. They called him Elvis because he never took off his sunglasses and wore the collar of his shirt turned up.

They called their headquarters, "the house." They had an unusual way of referring to their precincts. For example, if the police officers were based at the station house in the 17th precinct, they would say they were "out of the one-seven." Someone from the 21st precinct was from the two-one. A fellow officer not in their precinct was called "on the job."

"He's on the job, out of the two-one."

Veteran police officers were slightly paranoid. Upon reflection, I now think the paranoia was probably justified. When they would stop for coffee at a coffee shop, they would choose a table where they could sit with their backs to the wall. The table also had to afford them an unobstructed view of the cash register. They knew that the register was the most likely object to be "hit" in a robbery and they didn't want to have their backs to the action when a robbery went down.

I have to admit that it was a bit unnerving to sit with these guys sipping coffee and have them talk to you out of the sides of their mouths while their heads were turned to the cash register.

"I've got to pull a double today. I'm working a detail at the UN. The golfer's giving a speech." I learned later the police officer was referring to President Ford, who not only had a history of tripping and falling down, but had recently hit an innocent bystander with a wildly errant golf ball while playing in a charity event.

Once nicknamed, you carried the name forever. To this day, when I see a retrospective of past presidents or see the living presidents assembled at a state funeral, I see Clinton, Bush, Carter and the golfer.

I learned that cops can dispatch you with just a few words. They do it all the time. The night when Son of Sam had been captured and jailed, I had to call the chief of detectives to try to get more information for the early editions of the morning papers. The chief had been on the phone dealing with reporters for hours and was tired of our questions and pleas for more information.

I was particularly aggressive on the phone. I finally said, "Look, I have to get a new quote from you, Chief. I'm on deadline." And he said, "Well, I'm not," and hung up the phone. It was a lesson I carry with me to this day when I am talking to officials about a breaking news story. My time is not their time.

By the way, the cops had a nickname for me too.

"Drop 'Jimmy Breslin' here at the News and then swing by the house," they would say. (Jimmy Breslin, for those who don't know or remember, was New York City's most famous Pulitzer-prize-winning columnist and crime writer, and the author of "The Gang Who Couldn't Shoot Straight.")

Needless to say, I was flattered by the nickname.

But enough of all that. I've got to go commit journalism. I'm on deadline.

26.

ROAD NOT TAKEN:
STOMACH CRUNCHES

Summer is coming and we had better be ready to hide our stomachs. The only person who is truly happy about the coming heat is bare-midriff pop star Christina Aguilera. She possesses the most well-known stomach now that Britney Spears is pregnant. Even slouching in an arm chair on a talk show, she casts an aura of stomach slenderness.

The rest of us are more likely to have abdominal brethren among certain sun-bathing seals, happy walruses and submarine-slow manatees. Those of us who have held more gym memberships than mutual funds know that years of driving desks do not six-pack abs make.

Can you imagine what it takes to have a well-defined midsection? Well, this is the regimen recommended by certain abdominal training specialists: an hour each day of stomach crunches, sit-ups, lateral side twists until your muscles "burn." This is followed by two hours each day of generalized resistance exercise for the rest of your body. On top of the in-gym exercises are cardiovascular aerobic exercises for another hour spent each day running on the roads and byways of your town. On weekends, it is recommended that we augment our daily training with hours of vigorous kayaking, indoor rock climbing or marathon swimming.

Underpinning all this exercise is a nutritional regimen of high-fiber, low-carbs, green-is-great foods that put the rip in ripped and the cuts in cut. You do this for two consecutive years and you are slim but you still don't have a chiseled stomach. It takes two more years and then you have one of the six-pack abs - only one. The other five you will never have, or so your DNA seemingly decrees.

So this is why we're manatees. Most of us stop going to the gym in about two months. The running is about as regular as the siting of a pair of cardinals and the only unaided sit-up we do is the one required to get out of bed.

Nutritionally, doughnuts rule. We supplement our meatball subs and double whoppers with biggie fries and soft drinks the size of inverted traffic cones. During the day we take a few hits from frosted lattes, double espressos and coolata drinks made from caloric substances that could fuel a nuclear reactor.

So it is not surprising that, each summer, we find ourselves sitting in a beach chair under an umbrella with a shirt loose enough for an NBA center to wear without restricting his ability to dunk the ball - no make that - loose enough to hide the ball.

So here is our toast to Christina (and male hip hop stars like Usher who have the much-coveted ripped abs): Congratulations, and, oh, stay off our beach.

27.

BEE GEES AND WORDS ARE ALL WE HAVE

The best time to see and hear a live concert is to watch a taped one.

The Public Broadcasting System (PBS) airs concerts when they are raising funds. Because fund-raising appeals occur almost all the time now, a massive amount of air time needs to be filled. That makes for a ton of Three Tenors, or is it three tons of tenors? (Although I do admit, I never tire of hearing Andrea Bocelli's soaring voice filling the top-gallant sails of his vocal Tall Ship. We can see him gliding across the sea because it was "time to say goodbye."

Listening to a Bee Gees concert recently on PBS (out of nostalgia, not that I am a diehard Bee Gees fan), I was struck with the following: How many hit songs they wrote (They recorded more than 1,100 - "You should be dancing," "To love somebody," "Islands in the stream," "Lonely days," "Stayin' alive," "How deep is your love;" (They really did "own" the 1970s); how sad those songs were (Most of them dealt with loss); and what an incredible falsetto voice Barry Gibb has; (How does he manage to jump an octave or more , seemingly at will?).

The Bee Gees are described as an Anglo-Australian group because they emigrated to Australia in the 1950s and returned to Britain in 1967. One certainly can hear a trace of that amalgam of accents when they sing.

Robin, who wears the cool blue sunglasses that British rock stars seemed to have championed over the years, has an almost baleful voice. It actually quavers. It is especially effective when he sings songs like "I Told a Joke."

Maurice, Robin's fraternal twin brother, who died last year, sang understated and almost unnoticed harmony but looked cool in his black hat, shades and Western long-rider coat. But the focus ever since young Andy Gibb's death at 30, due to an overdose of drugs, has been on brother Barry. Barry wrote many of the songs that have secured the Bee Gees' international reputation. They were ballads and love songs and contained "old-fashioned" lyrics. By that, I mean words that had meaning and made sense and could stand on their own.

There is a line from "Words," written by Barry, Mo and Robin, that crystallizes the plight of someone desperately seeking the love of another: *It's only words, and words are all I have to take your heart away.*

Then there are these two stanzas from "Night Fever," now forever associated with John Travolta:

Listen to the ground,
there is movement all around,
there is something going down
and I can feel it.
On the waves of the air,
there is dancing out there,
If it's something we can share,
we can steal it.

And, for me, as a newspaperman, the following lines from "Stayin' Alive," are particularly intriguing:

And now it's all right, it's OK.
And you may look the other way.
We can try to understand
the New York Times' effect on man.

I am still trying to understand that effect.

Many thanks to the two surviving brothers of the Brothers Gibb, Barry and Robin. For both of whom, the lines from "Night Fever" are so appropriate:

Here I am,
praying for the moment to last
living on the music so fine,
home on the wind,
making it mine.

28.

ON WIPER BLADES, MECHANICS AND THE GRAMMAR OF LIFE

There are a few things in life that no one has as yet solved: Getting a car to last longer than its warranty, finding a cheap cellular telephone service provider, getting a printer/copy machine to work and being able to change your own windshield wiper blades.

Cosmic things all, but let me focus on the latter. As I have written in this column before, my luck with vehicles, safety inspections, and auto maintenance is like dealing with the common cold — just as I think I am immune to illness, a new strain of a virus appears and attacks my anti-bodies like locusts on lettuce.

So it was this week when I went to an auto specialty store and bought a pair of fancy new wiper blades to install on my car. The old blades had worn out and I needed non-streaky new ones to pass state safety inspection, whose deadline comes in a few days. (I don't know why I leave this stuff to the last minute. I plead newspaperman. I need deadlines to motivate me, I guess.)

Anyway, the specialty store has strict rules about not working on your car in its parking lot. They cite insurance regulations, lease restrictions from their landlord and bad karma. So I drove home with my new blades — one 20 inches long for the driver's side, the other 18 inches long for the passenger's side. I examined the device holding the blade to the wiper arm. It had more rust than the bridge of the Titanic. The little clip device that one "simply unclips" to remove the blade as the directions indicated wouldn't budge. I tried using a small screwdriver to pry it off. I attacked it with a pair of needle nose pliers that looked like a close-up shot in the horror movie the Arachnids. I even tried WD-40, heat from a torch and vice grips. I uttered loud oaths that scared my neighbors and caused several in-house dogs to bark.

After 67 minutes I gave up. I threw the new blades on the seat of my car and went to a gas station that I used to go to for minor repairs 10 years ago. Behind the gas pumps, I drove past idling diesel dump trucks, landscape trucks pulling trailers that held 79 rider mowers and abandoned wheel rims. It was an obstacle course. If you want to talk to the mechanic, well, buddy, you have got to get to him first. After waiting for him to put down the air hose with which he was blowing dust from a brake drum, I caught his eye.

Amazingly, even after about 10 years of driving by his station without stopping, but always waving at him, he recognized me. At one time I had brought four aging vehicles to him to fix — on an almost biweekly basis. Anyway, he came out and immediately looked at the new blades I had handed him and then at the car's wiper arms. "Can't be done," he said. "Someone has converted these blades with universal adapters and the springs are snapped off and the whole adapter is rusted on." My spirits sunk. The mechanic heard my audible sigh over the idling diesel trucks and went back into the garage. He returned with a heavy ratchet handle.

"What on earth is he going to turn with that big thing?" I thought. Well, he took the ratchet and started hitting the adapter. After several George Foreman blows the whole contraction flew off and landed on the faded hood of my car. Then, in a swirling movement that would impress Merlin, he magically snapped on the new blade. It was over.

Furthermore, and I want to tell the world this, he didn't charge me anything. I was willing to pay him a bag of Krugerrands, but, no, he wouldn't accept a dime. "You're a friend and a good customer," he said. I thanked him once more and wound my way back to the street. I was grateful and a little sad. It made me wish for an equivalent in my own profession.

"I'm sorry, sir, but these verbs are all worn out. I will have to replace them with some active transitive ones but they should last you way beyond your present rhetorical journey." Or, "I'm sorry but these nouns aren't up to code. They are out of round and thin and won't convey the precise meaning you need to get your points home safely."

I dreamed about shoring up dangling participles, welding split infinitives and redirecting misplaced modifiers as I drove home. When I got to my driveway I activated the arm that squirted windshield washer fluid on the windshield and watched the new wipers sweep away a mini-snowdrift of yellow pollen. Yes, this is the way it should be. Happiness is a pair of new windshield wipers.

29.

ON BUYING GIFTS FOR THE HOLIDAYS

It's October so we are preparing for the holiday. But the holiday my family has in mind is not Halloween - it's Christmas. That's right, while other families are out looking for the most symmetrical pumpkin, we're loading in rolls of holiday wrapping paper.

Giving a thoughtful gift is important and says a lot about a person. My dearly departed mother believed it was crucial to give at least one thing that she had made with her own hands. If the gift didn't require at least 1,000 hours of knitting, crocheting or sewing, then it wasn't a worthy gift. Many were the holiday seasons when I would receive an Afghan coverlet that was larger than a double bed or a matching woolen watch hat, with mittens and an accompanying six-foot-long scarf.

And I got some wonderful sweaters. Wait a minute. Let me stop writing this so I can go over to my dresser and pull out the sweater my mother knitted for me 25 years ago. OK, I'm back and wearing a dark brown woolen sweater that my mother custom tailored for me. I wanted the sweater to be really long so that it would not ride up over my waist when I was working outside. So she knitted in an extra long waist and designed the sweater to fit my torso with just the right amount of room to move about without that tourniquet-tight feeling you get from some store-bought sweaters.

Now, that is a thoughtful holiday present that I still cherish.

My brothers and I, however, practice a different holiday gift-buying strategy. Unlike my wife and her family who end their gift-buying by the first week in October, we feel that procuring the right Christmas gift is like a basketball game: You have until the last 2 seconds to make the crucial shot. One way to forecast what you might receive as a gift from one of us, is to examine what is available at the cash registers at department, retail and convenient stores on Christmas Eve.

We have been known to give only impulse-buy presents: flashlights, battery packs, chocolate samplers, cans of WD-40 (my family's equivalent of Windex in the film, "My Big Fat Greek Wedding") and soap opera magazines. All these items somehow mysteriously find their way under our Christmas trees. There is a disturbing interchangeability to our gifts: My gift to my brother could easily be given to my sister-in-law and vice versa.

But in my wife's family, holiday gift buying becomes a quest for everyone's personal Holy Grail. It is not unusual for one of them to surprise me with a first-edition, autographed book from one of my favorite authors or a small, museum-collectible antique that would make the Keno brothers swoon.

The gift certificates to Land's End that I give my family, in contrast, somehow lack the thoughtfulness of presents from my wife and my in-laws.

I think my brothers and I have holiday gift giving performance anxiety. We are afraid that the gift we think is wicked cool actually is not only ill-suited but pedestrian. Therefore, we don't take any risks but habitually fall back into the interchangeable-gift syndrome.

Thankfully, we have very forgiving relatives. They know how holiday-challenged we are and they ooh and ahh on Christmas morning: "That's great, Peter. Thanks. You can never have enough Armor-All polish these days. That's for sure."

I think this year, I will switch from Land's End to L.L. Bean. That way, the people to whom I give gifts will at least be able to get something a bit more exotic, like - I don't know - how about those cool-looking aluminum-framed snowshoes on page 96?

30.

Winter sport:
Battery jump starting

The cold snap we had at the beginning of the week was perfect weather to work inside my semi-heated garage. There is something calming about working with wrenches, especially when one is used to constructing things with nouns and verbs every day.

I chose my wrench time on a cold day to load-test the batteries in my vehicles to see whether they could make it through the winter. I have a "heavy-duty" battery tester. (Heavy duty means it's made from metal rather than plastic.) The tester has a big resister inside it surrounded by a heat shield. One simply connects the "heavy-duty" battery clips to the battery posts, presses the load switch, which places the load resister in series with the battery, and then one releases the button and takes a reading. If the meter needle falls in the green zone, the battery is fine but if it falls in the red zone it means you have to leave the heated garage and go out and buy a new battery.

There is a cardinal rule (which cardinal I don't know) of automotive electrical work which states when jump starting or trickle-charging a battery, always attach the red (positive) cable first and then the negative or black cable last. Also, when you are working on your car and you want the car's engine to be disabled and you want no voltage to flow through any of the wiring or any of the metal parts of the vehicle, one disconnects the negative (ground) cable first.

The negative battery cable is like Marshal Matt Dillon of the old radio and TV show, "Gunsmoke." He's the first person you call and the last person you want to see.

My three batteries passed the test so I charged them up to full capacity with my three (yes, I have three) chargers. I have one professional 250-amp model on wheels of which I am particularly proud. I tend to cart it out of the garage and then roll it back in when the neighbors are outside in their yards. I want them to see I have a macho charger that could bench press 450. (How's that for a mixed metaphor of pounds and amps?)

In fact, in the high-amp charging/starting position one can hear the electrolyte in the battery boiling like a tea kettle. I am not sure how harmful a whitewater of boiling acid is rushing over the relatively fragile metal plates in the battery, but I know enough not to keep the battery boiling too long. I usually turn the charger down to a gentlemanly 10 amps, which is usually enough current to bring even a weak battery up to full charge in a couple of hours.

I also own two battery boosters, which consist of a small, dry, transportable battery that you can charge from a wall outlet. You simply carry the booster, which is the size of a computer laptop on junk food, over to the vehicle that contains the dead battery, connect the cables, and jump start the vehicle. These are handy devices because you don't need a second vehicle and you don't have to struggle with serpent-like cables that would ensnare Laocoon. (If you get this ancient reference, please e-mail me at pcosta@cnc.com. I am conducting a survey about literary references. So far, no one under 50 has gotten the aforementioned reference, but I am not clever enough to think of a more modern metaphor using pop singer Beyonce, at least not one that doesn't contain embarrassing double entendres.)

Also, remember that car batteries with a five-year warranty usually die on the last day of the fourth year, summer or winter, usually at night on a deserted road where UFOs have previously been sighted.

31.

CLOWNS, COLUMNS AND ART HOPPE

It is not true that clowns are the saddest people in the circus.

Actually, clowns are fairly well-adjusted. It's just that clowning around and making people laugh on demand is a very taxing job. Writing this column is like clowning, except I don't wear any face paint or floppy shoes. Not before Thursday, that is.

Being silly is serious. It also involves considerable personal risk. Do you know what it is like to watch a family member read your column with a furrowed brow like a loan officer at a bank? Or the acid reflux one feels after discovering a typo in a published column? (Last week, I typed "Peter Jenkins" instead of "Peter Jennings." I heard about it right away - and not from Canadian readers either.)

I even had one reader write me to tell me I make too many parenthetical remarks. (What does he know? I like parentheses. They are ice tongs that grab a thought that was too late to include in the sentence before it.)

People often ask me which column of mine got the most laughs. The very first one I ever wrote got the most laughs. (I know, I should have stopped while I was ahead.) I was a graduate student at the University of California in Berserkley - as we used to call it then during the times of the great upheavals of student protests - and I had the good fortune to have a humor writing tutorial with legendary San Francisco Chronicle humor columnist, Art Hoppe.

Hoppe is no longer with us but is in that special place with humor writer S.J. Perlman and Evelyn Waugh and all the other humor masters. He was an elegant satirist. He was also an extremely good reporter in his day. His most famous news lead sentence, according to the San Francisco Chronicle, dealt with the marriage of Yankee baseball slugger Joe DiMaggio to sex icon Marilyn Monroe. Hoppe wrote:

"Joltin' Joe DiMaggio wedded the girl of his and many other men's dreams yesterday."

As a reporter, he also wrote a moving piece about an execution.

"They came to see Burton Abbott die," he wrote. "There were 53 of them — official witnesses. All were men. Women are not allowed to see a condemned man die ... . They gathered in front of the main gate to San Quentin at 9 a.m. yesterday. No one was late."

According to the Chronicle, when one of his columns generated a particularly ill-tempered letter he wrote back this response:

"The cookbook you have ordered will arrive under separate cover."

He taught me many things about humor writing, the most important of which was not to go for the easy joke but to let the thought cook in the creative oven like a soufflé. (Easy for him to say and do. Not so easy for the rest of us mortals who seemed to be addicted to fast food humor.)

Anyway, my first published humor column, which I wrote under Hoppe's tutelage, dealt with how college admissions people were looking for the absolutely ideal candidate. That ideal, sought-after student likely had an internship as an assistant surgeon, scored perfect 800s on the SAT and could play any woodwind or stringed instrument. Later in the column, I gave an example of a sample application letter, which caused guffaws throughout the newsroom from my colleagues and generated many letters from readers. I don't know why people at the time found that column so funny. I guess it mirrored what was going on during those days and rang true on some level.

It appeared in a Massachusetts newspaper and I sent a copy of the column to Hoppe. Ever the gracious mentor, he sent me a haiku-short letter:

"Absolutely lovely. Costa, this field isn't big enough for the both of us."

What a kind thing to say to someone like me just starting out in newspapers - even if his praise was exaggerated. I had the letter framed and now keep it as a cherished memento.

But getting back to clowns. I once asked Hoppe about clowning and the role of the literary clown. He said people kept expecting him to be funny spontaneously at parties. "I'm not that funny in person. I am funniest when I am behind a typewriter - after a long time behind a typewriter. Then, I'm funny but only until the next column."

How very true. His remark reminds me of my two favorite animal species who, unlike humans, seem to be funny all the time - elephants and pug dogs. (What, again with the elephants, you ask? I can't help it. They're cool and "The Lion King" production is in Boston yet again diverting the true respect elephants deserve to some growling, show-off, little lion.) Elephants and pugs are natural clowns. Can you imagine the ironic columns a wise, 70-year-old elephant could write? Can't you just see a pug reading them with those thoughtful Winston Churchill eyes?

By the way, next week my column should be funny/funnier. I have an idea for it and I am letting it cook.

32.

ON GASOLINE PRICES AND GIANT VEHICLES

Gasoline apparently is the only commodity that does not obey the law of supply and demand.

It seems that every time we go to the pumps the prices are slightly higher than the last time we filled up. This phenomenon occurs whether there are oil tankers clogging all the harbors on the East Coast or whether there is a solitary tanker just leaving the Strait of Hormuz with seven barrels of crude oil and a quart of extra, extra, ultrafine virgin olive oil. (Understanding olive oil labels requires a Ph.D. in organic chemistry and a knowledge of the black arts of alchemy. But that's another story.)

With a precision of movement that would impress Isaac Newton, gas prices go up during the summer precisely when we need gasoline the most. Now on the surface this may seem logical and consistent with the law of supply and demand. The more a commodity is needed but is scarce, the higher its price. Well, no one will say definitively that gasoline is scarce. In fact, there are some experts who say there is enough gasoline at present to meet demand. So, why do the prices rise when supply is still greater than demand?

I blame the Hummer. This giant SUV gets about 6 miles per gallon and people are driving them everywhere. Desperate 108-pound housewives get ladders and climb into their 3-ton Hummers to drop off 2-ounce letters at the post office. Their husbands drive to work in vehicles named for huge regions - Yukon, Dakota, etc. - and sit idling in traffic generating more greenhouse gasses than some island nations.

Everyone in the family simply must have his or her own muscle vehicle. Driveways have become tarmacs for wide-body cars and trucks waiting to take off to the mall or the convenience store. Filling up their tanks requires taking out an equity line of credit.

Hybrid fuel-electric cars that get 50 miles per gallon or more are still prohibitively expensive and only a small percentage of drivers are willing to give up their tanks for such econoboxes. In fact, I predict that quad-cab trucks will soon become even larger behemoths with numbered seats just like a Boeing 747.

I remember the gas line days of the Arab Oil Embargo of 1973-74 and the public that responded to the crisis by buying and driving small, fuel-efficient cars. Inflation then was horribly high, 8.5 percent, and industrial economies became more and more dependent on imported oil for their continued growth and success. On October 17, 1973, the Organization of Petroleum Exporting Countries imposed an oil embargo against the West in retaliation for Israel's pushing back the attacks from the armies of Egypt and Syria in the so-called Yom Kippur War.

Crude oil before the embargo cost $3 per barrel and jumped to $5.11 overnight. It rose to $11.65 by January of 1974. After the embargo, the price quadrupled from 30 cents a gallon to the then unheard-of price of $1.20 per gallon.

The difference this time is that the Saudis are pumping extra oil and U.S. and Coalition forces control Iraq's oil fields. In addition, the United States has the ability to receive 2,000,000 barrels per day from the Trans-Alaskan oil pipeline, which was completed in 1977. Today, debate continues over whether Mideast instability necessitates oil drilling in the Arctic Wildlife Refuge.

So, history tells us that soaring oil prices can throw us back into a serious recession like 1973-74. But this time, people don't seem likely to rediscover the 4-cylinder compact car. Ask anyone driving an Expedition or an Explorer or another E-vehicle. Like the supertankers that fuel them, it takes an enormous amount of time and whole oceans to turn around our big-vehicle mania.

See you at the pumps.

33.

SUMMERTIME AND THE GRILLING ISN'T EASY

It is easier to achieve cold fusion than it is to get a charcoal-fired grill up to operating temperature.

When I manage to get a fire hot enough to cook hamburgers, the fire is usually about 5 inches too low from the grill grate. Some nefarious grill designer decided long ago that all charcoal grills should require 1 and ½ bags of charcoal to work properly. I am usually about ½ bag short of enough charcoal to fill the grill up.

After years of shouting at the sky — and scaring the birds and squirrels who had gathered to smell the tantalizing aromas of hot dog and hamburger meat — I learned that I must buy two bags of charcoal at one time. That way, I will have enough charcoal for one grill session. Buy two, use 1 and ½. Remarkably, defying the laws of math and physics, that left over ½ never seems to amount to enough for the next grill session. No matter how many ½ bags I save, I end up buying two bags to use 1 and ½ anyway.

Grill timing requires the accuracy of an atomic clock. I am usually off by an hour. Even when I delay putting the food to be cooked on the grill by 45 minutes, I discover that only after cooking the food is the grill really ready to put out the most BTUs. Yes, I wait until the charcoal is all uniformly gray and radiating distributed heat but it still seems that there is some hidden grill-weight-control thermostat switch that kicks in when there is absolutely nothing on the grill: The second I take the cooked meat off the grill, the charcoals remarkably emit an intense, white heat.

I have resorted to the latest digital technology and bought a grill thermometer to tell me when the grill is hot enough to cook meat. I even have those pop-up wellness detection devices that I stick into steaks. They come in different caloric classes: rare, medium and well. When they pop up, the meat is allegedly cooked the specified amount. They seldom work. I remember forgetting one on the grill after cooking some steak and it popped up just after the 11 p.m. evening news

— frightening those same squirrels and birds who had come back to feast on any crumbs dropped from the afternoon's picnic.

I also have all manner of barbecue tongs and flipping devices but having them is like owning a great set of golf clubs - one still needs to be able to swing them. I fumble with the tongs, which just put the objects of my culinary desire 18 inches further away. I would have better luck using a symphony conductor's baton than I would with the stainless steel tongs. They numb my fingers and make me feel as if I am on an extravehicular space walk trying to put a battery in a wristwatch wearing gauntlet-size gloves somewhere above the Indian Ocean.

And even though I oil the grill, the meat always seems to stick. Turning over a hamburger requires two sets of tongs and a dexterity seen only in world-class brain surgeons.

The encouragement-criticism from the grill bystanders is very annoying too. My grill work has somehow become a very exciting spectator sport. People even bet on whether I can turn over a burger on only one try. They always win.

I used to try to cook the food to my guests' specifications and their individual timing needs but soon discovered that Bill decided to have another beer and wasn't ready for his medium burger and Jane had decided she was still working on her lemonade and wasn't ready for her rare steak and Robert decided he didn't want meat at all and would just have another helping of potato salad. To overcome this guest indecision, what I do is cook a bunch of hamburgers and hot dogs and put them on serving trays and tell the guests they can administer to their own steaks and that the grill is now theirs.

Then I hand over the tongs, pick up a drink and feel like Atlas without the globe.

Ah, yes, welcome to the summertime grilling season.

34.

SPLENDOR IN THE GRASS

I admit that I equate yard work with prison yards: It is that place where you are forced to exercise for a given period every day and you are never done until it snows and the yard is closed. There is also another similarity, and that is my yard - alias, my lawn - has the same trampled look as many yards at penitentiaries. Blame it on the nocturnal wildlife.

My lawn sports several rectangular areas that look as if someone has randomly turned over the turf with a jack hammer. I telephoned the town animal control officer to inquire what kind of animal was churning through my lawn and she said "skunks." Skunks? "Yes, skunks." It seems they like to eat the grubs that lie beneath the lawn in spring.

Well, one early pre-dawn morning a few days after the call to the animal control officer, I went out to retrieve the newspaper. It is "delivered" by a man, who identifies himself only as Sergei. Sergei drives a white station wagon with one brown door on the driver's side and throws the paper out his window. You can hear the newspaper hit the pavement followed by the sound of rubber squealing as the car speeds off into the pre-dawn blackness. You can hear the car's blown muffler bellowing for blocks.

After picking up the newspaper at the end of my driveway this dark morning, I walked back to the house and spied something on the lawn so huge it could have appeared in the ring on World Wrestling Entertainment's "SmackDown." It was a skunk. It was so big, it waddled. When it saw me it paraded nonchalantly over my lawn and into the woods.

So this was the nocturnal lawn destroyer, eh? Well, let's hope there are enough grubs for him or the asphalt shingles will be next, I said out loud, maintaining my reputation in the neighborhood as the strange guy who is up when he should be asleep and asleep when he should be up and who talks to himself.

The next day I decided to surf the Internet and find out how to deal with skunks. All the remedies carried so many cautionary warnings that I quickly determined it was easier to dispose plutonium than it was to risk exposure to the devastating spray from a skunk. Luckily, the skunk issue was really not the problem.

A couple of days later, just after leaving for work, I remembered I had left my sunglasses on the kitchen table. So I turned my car around and drove back into the driveway and there were three crows happily drilling through the topsoil of my lawn retrieving worms and grubs. They were having a wonderful time.

I got out of my car and stamped my foot on the sidewalk. I don't know whether crows smile or not, but I think they merely smiled at me and kept on excavating my lawn in search of the mother of all grubs.

This would not do. I immediately went to my lawn and garden shop and came home with chemical sprays that are supposed to help kill grubs and also make the grass unpalatable to birds. Well, the crows treated the chemicals like salad dressing and continued to peck through the lawn until all the grubs were gone. They then flew over a few houses away and started to work on the unkempt lawn of a neighbor whose yard work expertise makes me look like the host of PBS' "Victory Garden."

Well, anyway, once the crows left, I was able to start the annual spring yard cleanup and preparation work. The lawn in the back of my house is shaded by two towering oak trees that provide lovely shade during July but which drop branches and twigs throughout the winter. These branches seem to have woven themselves into a kind of wooden trampoline. When I would pick up one branch, a hundred other ensnarled branches would vibrate like a giant arboreal net. Gosh, what would happen if the tyrannosaurus skunk were to get trapped in this wooden web? The property would be uninhabitable for months, I said aloud once again.

I couldn't worry about that now because I had hours of back-breaking pick-up-sticks work to do. After a few Saturdays of clean up, it was finally time to put lime down on the lawn. This process, I am told, is a sure sign that the lawn owner doesn't know what he or she is doing. Experts say most fertilizing and conditioning work is done in the fall. Springtime is when you do a little spreading of chemicals to prevent things like grubs from infecting your lawn.

Anyway, lime spreading is kind of fun. You can throw this white powder everywhere, get your shoes covered with the stuff, as well as ruin a good pair of jeans. But there is something very primordial about throwing lime around. It just feels right even though it is wrong.

Well, amazingly, in a few weeks, my lawn will have recovered from the Hitchcock crows and my lime treatments and there will be grass to be mowed. I am one of the few people in the neighborhood who does not have a riding lawn mower, tractor or lawn service. I simply pull the cord on my lawnmower, hope it starts, and walk behind it, row after row after row until it runs out of gas.

I have often thought that I have reached the age when I should be piloting one of those fancy zero-radius riding mowers. I could wear the baseball cap that guys my age wear, keep a can of soda in the soda holder on the right fender and wear a short-sleeved shirt buttoned all the way up. Ever notice that old guys not only drive with their left directional signals permanently on but also button the top button on their sports shirts? Well, that will be me, perhaps next year. Skunk and crows not withstanding, I will be all buttoned up with no place to go but my yard.

35.

LIFE IN THE FAILED LANE

I was traveling down Route 2 the other day cruising at about 45 miles per hour when I saw blue strobe lights from a state trooper's car in my rearview mirror. I pulled over hoping he would drive by and apprehend a real felon, but, no, the lights were for me.

I put the vehicle shift lever in park and reached over to try to open the glove box where I keep the vehicle's registration. I couldn't quite reach far enough so I unbuckled my seat belt for more range of motion. After I had done that I noticed that the state trooper was walking very slowly toward my vehicle the way police do when they think they have a fugitive in their sights.

Wait a minute, I thought. He's going to think I was not wearing my seat belt, which is required by state law and, whammo, he'll slap that fine on top of the ticket he will write for whatever reason he's stopped me in the first place.

I immediately started fiddling with the buckle to try to belt myself back in. Then I thought he would think I was trying to either hide a controlled substance or maybe that I was about to pull out a concealed weapon. Then I looked and saw that there was a vial of eye drops on the passenger seat and that maybe he would think it was some other kind of drug. Needless to say I was fidgeting and moving around very suspiciously.

I looked in my side mirror and to my great relief saw that at least he did not have his hand on the grip of his gun as he approached. Maybe it was the dress shirt and tie I was wearing that stopped him from drawing his weapon. Maybe it will be a minor, white-collar infraction he is pulling me over for, I thought, like failing to put a stamp on a utility bill envelope or overdue books from the regional lending library.

"May I see your license and registration please?" he asked.

With slightly shaking hands, I handed both over to him. He looked at the license and said, "Do you know why I pulled you over?" I wanted to say, "For my continued support of the State Police Retirement and

Welfare Fund?" But knowing that would lead to handcuffs, just said, "No, officer, I don't."

"Well, your inspection sticker has expired. Did you know that?"

"Yes, I was going to get the vehicle inspected tomorrow," I said.

"Sorry but yesterday was the last day of the grace period for inspecting your vehicle. Let me check this registration out and I'll be right back," he said and walked back to his cruiser.

I know I should have said I was en route to the inspection station just as he stopped me but I didn't. I don't know why I was so dumb. I immediately blamed my bad luck.

How did the state trooper spot the elapsed sticker when I was traveling at speed on the highway surrounded by a cluster of cars? He would have had to redirect the Hubble Space Telescope to see the number on the sticker.

Why me? Other guys drive their cars with a tail light burned out until their children graduate from college and never get stopped. Or they have defective headlights or stop lights that don't work at all or faulty directional signals or blown mufflers that make their cars sound like the liftoff of a Saturn-5 rocket. And yet, they drive on obliviously, their bass boosts pumping out a song so loud you can hear it through closed windows. (It's always a song you don't really want to hear.)

Once at a dreaded inspection station, I was informed that one of my two rear license plate illumination bulbs was burned out and that I was going to fail the inspection because of it. Can you imagine that? The bulb even at peak efficiency was designed to provide less illumination than a candle held on the Sea of Tranquility lunar landing site. And yet, one of these two little bulbs was out and so was my chance to pass inspection.

.I am the kind of guy who has a tire tread gauge which I use to see whether I have enough tread on the tires to pass inspection. I always do. I also jack up the front end and use a pry bar to check the suspension for excessive play.

But I am still the Rodney Dangerfield of car owners. An old Jeep that I owned contained gas tank straps that were starting to rust and I was informed that the vehicle would pass this time but next time the straps had to be replaced. Do you know how hard it is even to see the straps holding a tank in place? The vehicle has to be on a lift and you need a probe light from Jacques Cousteau's deep water submersible to get a view of it.

Once, one of my vehicles with only 12,000 miles on it failed inspection because of a ball joint that was slightly loose and over spec.

Next I expect the inspectors to say that the molecular structure of the steel holding the overflow water bottle to the radiator is deficient and doesn't contain enough crucial molybdenum for the longevity of the vehicle.

One final thought. Do you normally wait for the police officer to drive away after he hands you a ticket or do you pull out first? I pulled out first but not before carefully signaling my intentions with my working directional signal and looking at my flawless side mirror and accelerating my run-silent, run-deep muffler-quiet engine.

But I haven't checked my windshield visors lately. Are they up to spec? I have a feeling I will soon find out some night under blue lights.

36.

ROCKETS RED GLARE
AND OTHER WORK-RELATED NOISES

I don't like noise. My over-sensitivity to loud things may be a function of having spent a lifetime in newsrooms with people talking on telephones 36 inches away, with scanners squawking, with fax machines beeping and copy machines reproducing 2,000 copies of 6-column blank layout sheets.

Most of us have gotten used to this noise-over-noise audio tapestry. The white noise from the central air conditioning also helps. But none of us can deal with the shot-rang-out bang that we hear occasionally. The overnight package delivery people are legendary for this kind of noise.

An example of this is their performance with the sliding doors on their trucks. Now granted, the law of inertia dictates that a heavy door needs a lot of energy to get it in motion and even more energy to overcome the friction from the channel iron tracks in which it runs. However, there is no law of physics that says once the door is in motion that the driver should pull it down with the strength of Arnold Swarzenegger in his prime and on supplements.

I have watched drivers on the loading dock close their doors with such force that the door actually bounced back open by three feet like a heavy weight soaring to ring the gong at the strongman's sledgehammer event at a carnival.

Even more irritating is the cannonade they make with their wheeled hand trucks. Now most of the overnight-package delivery personnel have those lightweight magnesium hand dollies that can be configured to serve as a two-wheeled upright device or a four-wheeled platform. The drivers hurl these hand trucks to the loading docks like Cro-Magnons tossing wooly mammoths off cliffs. The trucks themselves back into the loading docks with resounding booms that mimic the Concorde as it passes through Mach 1 over the North Atlantic.

"What was that?" we all say in unison as the delivery guy backs his truck into the loading dock at 10:28 a.m., two minutes before the dreaded must-be-there-by-10:30 deadline.

We can expect loud noises at the workplace because it is difficult to do commerce without commotion. In the suburbs, however, when you lie in a backyard hammock ideally one only wants to hear the rustling of leaves and the singing of birds. I was lying in a rope hammock during the weekend when a car drove by with its sub-woofers pounding out a bass line so loud that it rivaled an outdoor Rolling Stones' concert.

As I write this at 7:15 a.m., a gigantic, praying mantis trash pickup truck rumbles outside my window. Even with the air conditioning on and police scanners squawking the morning roster call-up, "Car 3, Unit 6, Rescue 2, K-9," I could still hear the rumbling and the hydraulic lift noise right through the triple-paned windows.

Who designed these Erector Set trucks? The truck inserted its two antennae into a big blue dumpster and hoisted it over the cab in a giant arc. When it was over the bin area behind the cab, the driver pulled levers inside the truck to shake the bin to make sure everything fell out. It sounded like the shelling of Fort Sumter. Then it lowered the dumpster to the ground setting off seismic gauges in universities across the continent.

And as a fitting sonic coda, it pulled away with its diesel engine roaring and its gear box grinding. Trucks this large have twin axles and about 15 gears forward. It seemed to have shifted seven times before it reached about five miles per hour. I could hear the truck as it pulled out of the parking lot and could still hear it three streets away.

It all makes me wish for Maxwell's Smart's "Cone of Silence," on the old TV show, "Get Smart."

Oh, well, it's quiet now as I finish this - well, almost quiet. A voice hidden in a fax machine is saying that "we're sorry but the number you have dialed is not in service." It will do that three times and then wait five minutes and automatically redial the wrong fax number again.

Maybe by then I can go out to the loading dock and hold the door for the overnight delivery person.

37.

PROCRASTINATION:
WAIT, WAIT DON'T TELL ME

I don't have the luxury of having the services of a concierge. (Although my wife would say she has performed in that capacity for decades.) I can't say, "Pick up a quart of oil at the auto store and please have my truck inspected by this evening." So, I do the next best thing. I procrastinate.

As I drive to work I think of all the things I should have done before getting behind the wheel. I should have bought some cleaning solution for my steam iron. All the holes are plugged. The last time I tried my mother's method of putting vinegar in the iron, all I managed to accomplish was to destroy the electronic chip in the iron. It also caused Grace the pug dog to wrinkle her already-wrinkled forehead when she smelled the odor of burnt vinegar wafting through the house.

I look at the numbers on the pliable plastic oil sticker on the windshield. I have driven enough miles to have a close encounter with the planet Pluto. I don't need an oil change; I need a valve job. Maybe I can put the engine job off until spring.

On the passenger seat is a book to be returned to the library. I had taken it out of the library at about the time when VHS-format videos were still reigning supreme. Can you imagine the fine on this baby? Maybe I can say it was lost and pay for its replacement. Even at $25 it will be cheaper than a fine that is older than the Jurassic Era.

I have got to get air in the left front tire. I must have bent the rim when I went through a pot hole on the Route 2 lunarscape. The tire is leaking slightly - maybe a pound a week. I figure I have until Ground Hog's Day before I call AAA and have them come out and pump it up somewhere on the shoulder of Route 2, late at night in the rain.

I have got to get a tax form for the $362 sale of stock I made this year. Now, let's see, capital gains on that will be about the price of a half a tank of pre-Katrina gas.

Speaking of gas, I need to buy some for the snow thrower. I have got to remember to put the plastic can in the bed of my truck so I can stop after work and get five gallons of unleaded. I also need to get a new ice scraper. The last one snapped in the cold like a balsa wood model plane (remember those?) when it hit the heavy ice near the wiper blades. The wiper blades? Those are the two devices that are slowly etching a perfect semi-circle in the windshield. Next fill up I will replace them, for sure.

But I had better have cash with me. The last time I tried to put something on my oil company charge card, alarms went off all over Houston. Late payment does it every time. I have got to remember to pay them within two weeks of receipt.

Come to think of it, I haven't done anything within two weeks of receipt except go to the emergency room for chest pains. Even then, I waited a day to see whether they were real pains or imagined ones. By the way, forget what your mother told you. It is never "just something you ate." I have never been to a doctor who has said, "Don't worry, Peter, it is just something you ate." They usually say, "We've ordered a CAT scan and lab tests, because we think your symptoms are not related to digestion."

I think a little procrastination is a good thing. It is very New Age. Think of it as stopping to free your inner child as you smell the roses on the way to work listening to Gregorian Chants on Route 2.

Everything else can wait until tomorrow.

38.

PATH OF LEAST RESISTANCE
RESOLUTIONS

This is the time of year when we make our New Year's resolutions. They usually center on paying more attention to diet, exercising more, spending more time with family and reading one more good book than we did last year. (For all too many Americans, the number of books read in one year still remains one.)

Well, I'm tired of making resolutions that I cannot keep. I usually last two weeks on my New Year's diet; two days on abdominal crunches; two hours on not eating chocolate. But because of my profession, and the fact that I like books, I can honestly say I read many good books a year. Some I read because I think I should. Bill Clinton's unmercifully long autobiography is one such example.

By the way, I think Bill has delusions of being a capital-W Writer. He is definitely lowercase. Being glib verbally does not necessarily translate into compelling prose. He could have benefited from a ghost writer like Jack Kennedy's man, Ted Sorenson. Sorenson, if nothing else, knew how to power his prose with ancient Greek figures of speech like antimetabole: Ask not what your country can do for *you*; ask what *you* can do for your country.

How easily I get sidetracked. Back to my resolution on resolutions. I have decided to put into place my plan for Path of Least Resistance (PLR) for New Year's resolutions. (How about those alliterative p's in that sentence?) It would work like this: resolve to do better in small ways that you can realistically carry out.

Some examples:

I resolve not to interrupt the three people standing in a semi-circle blocking the door at Dunkin' Donuts talking about the problem of ice dams on their roofs and will not say to them: "For the sake of public safety, if for no other reason, would you mind moving over a few steps and not blocking this primary fire exit?"

I resolve not to interrupt the clerk at the convenience store who is talking on a cell phone with his back to the counter and will not say

"Hello, can the six of us in line check out now or would you like us to come back at a more convenient time for you?" (It is amazing I haven't been forced to duke it out in the parking lot after saying these caustic-toxic things to clerks.)

I resolve not to yell at the television set when they run a promo of their show just as the show is starting. We're already watching, so why promote an in-progress show? Do viewers really have a negative time-backwards attention span?

I resolve not to bore everyone about the absolutely endearing things our Pug dog did the previous night. I have to remember that not everyone melts the way I do when I play with a puppy.

I resolve not to spend four hours watching the game that is on before the Patriots game starts. I sometimes cannot even recognize the other teams from their helmets nut I still watch. Is that Tampa Bay or are they the Houston Oilers? (I know they're not called the Oilers anymore and that they moved to Tennessee in 1997.) And another of my peeve pets: How many football players are injured in celebration whacks to their helmets, chest bumps, piling on, etc., after they have just scored a touchdown? It looks more dangerous than running full tilt into Rodney Harrison.

I resolve not to tell journalism war stories about events that took place seven years before the person I am talking to was born. I remember having a teacher regale us (make that, re-gail as in wind) about how he covered the Suez Canal Crisis. He just as well as might have described how he covered Caesar's Gallic Wars. And yet, I find myself talking about how I helped write stories about the U.S. hostage crisis in Iran during the Carter Administration, my own Suez Canal crisis. That's Carter the carpenter of Habitat and Nobel Peace prize fame. (Actually, I confess I found my former teacher's Suez stories interesting simply because he grew so animated when he told us about them. It gave us a sense of the excitement of being close to history as it is being made.)

Finally, a resolution I know I will not keep:
I resolve not to live an over-examined life.

39.

LANGUAGE THAT PASSES MUSTER

I wrote a headline last week that used the old phrase, "whet your appetite." I was concerned because I thought many readers would think I had made a typographical error and inserted a wayward "h." The word, "whet," according to the tenth edition of Merriam Webster's Collegiate Dictionary, means "to sharpen by rubbing on or with something (as a stone)." It also can mean to make keen or more acute as in "whet your appetite."

This is not to be confused with the expression, "wet your whistle," which connotes pretty much the same thing but the wet is h-less.

I am not advocating recycling clichés but I think we should be able to have as many notes to play as possible in this music we call language. Ask any seventh-grader, it is quite possible to navigate through an entire day of conversation by just saying "awesome," "totally," "whacked," or "whatever."

Whatever.

You don't have to be a comedian like Robin Williams or a poet like Seamus Heaney to be known for using intriguing language. Think back to that teacher who made you laugh or that raconteur of an uncle who told such fascinating stories and you will recall it was the words and the unique presentation of them that you remember.

As I have written in this column many times, I agree that language should be allowed to change and evolve over the centuries, but I also think a lexicon of agreed-upon words and expressions should exist and that it should serve as the currency for our linguistic commerce.

I am struck by how many ancient-sounding phrases people of my generation use. Phrases like "pass muster." Just the other day, someone said that a report wouldn't "pass muster," to wit, would not stand up to critical examination and review. That phrase has been woven into our word tapestry from books we have read about the military, from hearing the phrase around the dinner table when we were growing up, and from peers who used words like those and others on the playgrounds, in the classrooms and at the malt shoppe. (Remember when there was an actual soda fountain, all stainless steel and shiny, that served concocted, sweet drinks?)

People of my boomer generation also know and use a lot of foreign phrases. French phrases like "raison d'être" (reason for being), "contretemps" (political setback); "détente" (relaxation of tensions) spice our talk and writing like garlic. Legions of Latin expressions march through our prose, "mirabile dictu" (wonderful to be told) and "ad infinitum" (to infinity). For some of us, the "ne plus ultra" (ultimate) of educated discourse is to deploy appropriately and perfectly a well-known Latin phrase in a letter or essay.

I always loved the phrases that derived from mythology. Just the other day I said, "And then the governor ruled on the case, 'deus ex machina,' and returned to his Olympus in Boston." In ancient Greek drama, a god was introduced by means of a crane or other mechanical device and was literally lowered to the stage to present a godly solution to a heretofore unsolvable human dilemma. It was the very definition of a contrived, i.e., mechanical, solution.

Now, of course, when I say something like deus ex machina to my buddies who are watching the NFL with me, I make sure I say it in a deep voice that a Spartan warrior might use. I have written about this curious American phenomenon before: Men who are literary are thought of as wimps. I say, "Oh yeah, ever read any Julius Caesar? Do you think he was a wimp?" And, "Wimp, eh? I'll arm wrestle you for that Coors Light but first let me put down my T.S. Eliot."

(An aside: if the NHL ever comes back, I think a fun new name for a hockey team would be "the Jersey Barriers." Also, a college senior told me he was graduating with a degree in computer science this May. His specialty? "Computer forensics." Cool. I can see it now: "CSI: Miami" spawns "CSI: Computer.")

I think it is fun and rewarding to have one's life enriched by the classical lexicon and by a reservoir of historical experiences and apt expressions. By the past, I mean not just the ancients but the 1960s and 1970s — Norman Mailer in his prime, Tom Wolfe of linen suit fame, Kurt Vonnegut in "Cat's Cradle," and Joan Didion on Salvador.

So many people today live in the real-time, digital present that anything with a half-life more than 15 minutes is automatically ruled obsolete. That's too bad. I wish we could spend less time on all things video and more time riding the waves of words.

Like, you know, totally. Words rule.

"Pax vobiscum." (Peace go with you.)

40.

CAR REPAIR BILL LIKE RANSOM NOTE

We don't maintain our cars these days, we rebuild them at random intervals. In the old days of carburetor-aspirated engines, all you needed to do was change the oil regularly, rotate your tires and try not to burn too much rubber when you and your buddies drove by the high school at noon. Now cars undergo a rebuilding process that rivals the airline industry in which engines are regularly rebuilt.

This fact of automotive life was arc-welded on to my consciousness by a bill I received from one of those nationally syndicated repair shops. I had brought my car in for an oil change and tire rotation (old habits die hard) and was informed that my car needed a bunch of must-do-now-or-suffer- immediate-rollover repairs. The "boot" that covers the CV (constant velocity) joint was cracked and dirt had gotten into the gears making the front drive shaft sound like a cement mixer mixing three parts gravel with two parts water.

Not only did I need both halves of the axle repaired but I also needed new disc brake pads, rotors reground and a new exhaust system from stem to stern. The estimated cost of these repairs looked like a phone number.

Now it takes a brave person to say, "OK, thanks for the recommendations, but please lower my car from the lift and I will go to four other garages for comparison repair estimates." It's just not done because it implies that you think the technicians with whom you are dealing are brigands, which in fact they are. More than 90 percent of the time, these guys perform work you really don't need at prices that would make the auditor of the Big Dig blanch.

Even the fast oil change places offer to replace things that really don't need replacing like PCV valves, windshield wiper blades, air filters and a host of emissions parts that are always grimy-looking, but more often than not, still in good-working order. The function of these parts is to filter air, fuel and gasses, so naturally there will be some grease and oil on their outsides.

Back to the garage bay brigands. But there you are, car on lift, repair estimate in hand. What do you do? You reach for a credit card and give them the go-ahead. Some of the reasons you accede to this ransom request is because you are already there, your car is on the lift and they promise they can "get you right out." Now, you are cheered by this news because normally when you call ahead and say you need x, y, and z done, they tell you they can see you next Shrove Tuesday or some other date in the astronomical, comet-pass-this-way future.

So you accede and let the work begin. After about seven hours in the waiting room watching daytime weekend television and reading magazines that are old even by podiatrists' standards, you get your car back and the paperwork that goes with it. If you look carefully, the only things that are guaranteed "for life" are the brake pads and the muffler. Everything else, pipes, clamps — anything made from ferrous metals — are not guaranteed at all. The guarantee excludes labor costs, of course. People have actually had transplant surgery that cost less than typical exhaust/brakes/axle repairs.

So, perhaps the thing to do is buy a new car that has a bumper-to-bumper warranty that you have had three lawyers, two auditors, and your cousin, Vinny, examine and approve. Then, when your car hits mega-miles, you trade it in for a new one with similar warranty. The only problem with that approach is that new cars depreciate faster than freon in your air conditioning system and that you lose about $10 per revolution of your tires. When you go to trade up to a new model you have lost more than half the cost of a new car in the time it takes between your first and second oil change.

There is no real solution to the car repair dilemma. You could take a month and drive your car to various repair shops for estimates of repair work needed but these days there are few shops that will give free estimates. Usually they charge an hour's worth of labor (at least $49.99) just to tell you what they think is wrong with your car. Then the multiplier effect goes into action and the bill climbs by the hundreds.

So, car owners are at the mercy of franchise owners who enjoy profit margins not seen anywhere outside the Gulf of Oman. Oh, well, at least the brake pads and the muffler are guaranteed for the "life of your vehicle." Labor and psychotherapy not included.

41.

FOR SOME, THE SILENCE OF EARLY RETIREMENT IS UNBEARABLE

He took early retirement recently. He accepted a company buyout at age 55 and said goodbye to all that. His wife continued to work because they needed medical benefits, at least until Social Security kicked in.

He had grand plans for his world-without-work years. He would travel, spend more time with his family and work on his hobbies, go to the gym more, enjoy leisure pursuits, stay up later and sleep longer.

The first six months went according to plan. He worked steadily in his woodworking workshop from early morning to late afternoon as he made bookcases, a chaise lounge for the patio and a Parsons table with intricate, hidden joints and angles. He was on a first-name basis at the gym with the trainers. He was taking more interesting and artful pictures with his non-digital 35mm camera. Some of the photos were actually very well-composed and almost arty.

He had just finished reading "The Da Vinci Code" almost two years after it was first on the best seller list.

Then he started to wander. He found himself having long conversations with the hardware store guy about tools, about how fasteners had changed over the years, how he was thinking of buying a small air compressor to run some simple power tools and inflate tires and air mattresses for the upcoming summer camping season.

At Dunkin' Donuts he was becoming known as the funny older guy who kids the help, almost all of whom are from Brazil, with his stories about having spent a week in Rio de Janeiro frequenting all the tourist spots near Ipanema Beach.

He got haircuts every three weeks now just so he could interact with humans. He missed the office chatter about the latest breaking news story, the Red Sox lineup changes and season prospects, movies and music. He even missed fashion. He used to make fun of the office talk that "gray was the new black" or that "winter white was making a comeback" or that super-pointy shoes were now the latest style for women and linen jackets without a back vent were still in style for men. Now he didn't even know how wide men's ties should be.

In his retirement, he had become, officially, out of it. Disconnected and on the fringe, he was now invisible.

He spent hours surfing Web sites he would not have even have clicked on before his retirement. He read junk mail about his college with the intensity and interest of a member of the board of trustees. He gave way to waves of nostalgia and was guilty of substituting a glossed-over past for four fairly unhappy college years. He even started to wear his college ring.

The noise of the present was very far away now, removed to downtown offices. Now he heard the wind, every now and then a passing delivery truck, but mostly just house noises.

He knew from the creaks and sighs of the furnace when the circulator motors were turning on to maintain an even heat in all the zones of the house, and when the dishwasher turned on using hot water and forcing the furnace ignition gun to fire and the blower to turn on.

When he walked the dog in the backyard, he often stopped and felt the bark of the trees. The knurled wood served as testimony to the utter indifference of the natural surroundings to his solitary life. He was lonely and alone and he felt trapped.

He telephoned his brother. "How is everything down there? Maybe we should get together when the weather gets better, what do you think? I could come down for a few days and we could go fishing on the bay and maybe eat some steamers, or take in a ballgame, what do you think?"

His brother was pleasant but had to beg off because he was traveling overseas on business for the next month and was too pressed to take any time off.

He would have called his daughter but she was making her own life now and didn't want to sit with her dad and listen to him talk about the past and his keen sense of loss. It was too depressing for her, so she tried to limit her time by just phoning him once a week.

He was at odds with himself. People — even mere acquaintances — started to detect an edge to his comments.

He slept fitfully and stopped going to the gym. He scanned Web sites for jobs in his field. The economy was slowly recovering but no company was busy enough or had enough major projects to be able to hire outsiders, certainly not ones with gray temples and long résumés. Not yet.

He became resigned that his work life was not only over but had been consigned to a time capsule of memories that only his immediate family would find interesting enough to dig up when he was gone.

He sat on his handcrafted chaise lounge and looked at the trees as they stretched toward the spring sun. He watched a cloud drift in from the west and gave his dog a pat on the head.

"Just you and me, now, boy," he said. "Let me tell you about the hang-gliders who jump off the hills and glide on to Ipanema Beach. They look like giant butterflies, floating, floating."

42.

STREAM OF CONSCIOUSNESS OVERFLOWS ITS BANKS

Here are some random, uncollected thoughts caused by mistakenly driving off to work at 3:46 a.m. due to Daylight Savings Time.

For the past few days I have been checking the NOAA river stage sites to monitor the rising waters of our region. Some of the towns in the Merrimack Valley area were "bursting" their banks by as little as three inches, while others were truly overflowing by several serious feet.

I immediately thought of former CBS anchorman, Dan Rather. He loved violent weather. He made television reporting history by allegedly chaining himself to a tree during a hurricane on the Texas Gulf Coast and broadcasting the sound and fury of the storm. And he did so as he spouted those Texas down-home phrases that so many people loved and hated.

In our present river case, I imagine he would say something about a watched pot never boils until you turn your back. (I just made that up; no, I am not related to Dan Rather and I have only been to Texas once in my life.) So there Dan stands, the rain slants in like rope, his safari shirt beats in the wind, his microphone picks up a freight-train of gusts and unmovable Dan signs off: "Dan Rather, in the eye of Hurricane, Houston."

Not to be outdone, NBC's recently departed Tom Brokaw would clearly see parallels with The Greatest Generation and marvel at how they coped — silently — with floods of the 1940s when they had to import natural rubber raincoats from Burma.

Peter Jennings of ABC didn't experience any floods in Canada so his coifed hair has stayed unmoved and lacquered for decades.

I enjoy making fun of the TV guys because I am clearly and rather painfully jealous. They earn more in a single end-of-year performance bonus than most of us on the print side have accumulated after decades of saving in our 401k's. And we got better grades all through school than they did.

But I still can't, aah, say a whole extemporaneous paragraph on camera the way they can without uttering a single aah. But I remember one incident when a highly paid TV guy borrowed my notebook and read it over the air, giving my news agency a rather softly spoken but legal acknowledgement at the end of his piece. At the time I was making per week what he was spending on his daily dry cleaning.

OK, moving right along. How about those Red Sox on opening day in the Bronx? Johnny Damon played like a genius instead of his usual idiot self. His fumbled catch in center field made Moe, Larry and Curly look athletic. But he has written an entertaining as-told-to book.

Why do people like to look into camp fires and fireplaces? (Wait a minute. I wrote about this in 1971, 1984 and 2003.) I have actually written something verbatim that I had written a decade or more ago and thinking it was fresh and new and cool. Really.

Also, why does getting a CV joint replaced in your car always seem to cost about $300 more than you expected? Car batteries must have a secret digital clock built into them that turns off exactly as the five-year warranty expires. Batteries last longer than five years only in Arizona and the Gobi desert.

The Literature of Loss, my favorite topic. If I start my own blog, I plan to call it the Literature of Loss Web site. It will get three hits from lonely guys in Naples, Manila and Brockton. I will invite comments about how we deal with the loss of loved ones, loss of health, loss of jobs, loss of style and loss of the wild spirit that used to dwell deep in our DNA. It will be a sad site.

My favorite line comes from playwright Edward Albee: For some, the dice have grown too big to toss.

I would like to put up a sign in the newsroom where I am writing this. It would say: Contents under pressure. HR wouldn't approve. They would urge me to call the confidential help line to try to cope with my stress. I would do that, but they would recognize my voice. Well, maybe not my voice, but certainly my aahs.

43.

REPORTING THE NEWS, PHRASE BY PHRASE

My best friend in graduate school in California was a Texan. He grew up in Beaumont. Tom (I called him Tom but his Texas friends all called him Tommie) looks like the stereotype of a Texan. He is tall and "lanky" and sits high in the saddle. He also possesses a sweet and accurate jump shot. When he would shoot, the basketball would leave his long fingers, arc gracefully to the hoop in a slow-motion parabola and spin through the net with a soft swish.

Tom's way of speaking, to my Eastern seaboard ears, was representative of someone definitely from the Lone Star State. But, interestingly, he used to make fun of my clipped accent and speed-dominated lifestyle. Having gone to college in new York City, I was forced to jettison my Massachusetts accent early. But I guess I still have an Eastern cast to my speech.

Tom laughed at the way I said the word, "Time," as in Time Magazine. He said I pronounced it "Tye-ehm," with an exaggerated sharpness to the "i" sound and an abrupt edge to the pronunciation of the letter "m." He used to pronounce Time slowly, and with what I thought was a drawl. For him the word was "Tahhmm."

Tom always tried me to get me to slow down – physically and mentally. He said I walked as if I had springs in my heels. He would walk in long, loping strides. I also had the bad habit of trying to finish his (and everyone else's) sentences until one day, he said, "No, I'm not going to say what you think, Peter. Actually, I was going to say this." From then on, I waited for him to finish his own thoughts and grew to understand and appreciate his insights.

We all were very full of ourselves back then. Armed with our degrees and reporting skills, we were going to newspapers across the country and write stories that would bust the town wide open. I tell the story of being one of two reporters serving as the news pool selected to interview then-governor of California, Ronald Reagan. I had prepared a list of questions that I thought would push the good governor back on his heels. But after talking with him and listening to what he had tried to do as governor to improve the plight of the poor, to improve public education, even to protect free speech — a big issue back then during the Free Speech Movement in Berkeley — we came away with a different, better impression of the man. We even thought he was a genuinely nice guy. Later on, after he became president, even his harshest critics would say Reagan was a disarmingly funny and folksy guy without any real malice.

So much for busting the town wide open with our stories. But it taught us a valuable lesson about harboring pre-conceived ideas about people and issues. Tom wasn't surprised. He knew politicians in Texas who were complex and multifaceted, had different views depending on what the issue was and who could not be portrayed with a simple label like liberal or conservative, Democrat or Republican.

A southern Democrat could be more conservative than a traditional Republican. Also, there is a tendency to label a public figure with a phrase and pigeon hole that person in the press. (An aside, I can remember editing copy on the General Desk of a wire service in New York City and seeing the phrase, "Panamanian strongman," in virtually every story we wrote about Manuel Noriega. Also, for almost a decade, reporters would write "the financially troubled Chrysler Motors," until Chrysler got their government bail out and later became profitable. Readers, it was thought then, like convenient "handles" for public figures and companies.)

Maybe it has something to do with headline writing and the art of saying something in short-hand. The Donald comes to mind as does Arnold, the Governator.

In any case, we have a penchant for the apt, summary epithet, even if it isn't entirely accurate or loses currency after someone's position changes or evolves.

Anyway, Tom would eventually return to Texas, and after years of reporting and editing stories about those Texas politicians he knew so well, would rise to the position of managing editor in Houston. He retired from daily journalism last year and has become a journalism professor back in California, the state where we both began our reporter's journeys.

I'm going to send him this column but he will be too modest to show it to his students. "We don't write about ourselves and we shouldn't become news," he would say.

He's right, of course, unless one is writing a personal column. I thought it was "teyem" to write this one.

44.

Beware 'sunny' Ides of March

I don't like sunny meteorologists who always look on the bright side of everything.

"Well, folks, the three-day blizzard is finally over and the snow totals are of truly historic proportions, but that monster storm is finally moving out to sea. Tomorrow, there will be lots of sunshine with really clear skies. There will be some wind from the northwest with gusts to about 30 or 35 miles per hour, so bundle up and remember to wear layers and a hat.

"The temperatures will start out near zero, but by mid-afternoon they will shoot up to the low 30s. Only six more weeks of winter and with all that sun today it looks like a great start to your morning."

Yes, it is a great morning if you are sitting inside a heated studio drinking hot cappuccino under tropical-like klieg lights. But stand outside in the parking lot with temperatures in the teens and with gales stronger than the winds buffeting Cape Horn, and then tell me what a great start to the morning it is.

Worse, are sunny mechanics.

"Well it isn't as bad as it could be. You definitely need new brake pads, new rotors and new calipers on the front, but the rear calipers look OK. So, just pads and rotors for the rear.

"The way you were describing the dragging, I thought it could be worse. You could have needed new brake lines, a new master cylinder, a new load-sensing valve, new backing plates and all new hardware. That would have cost you.

"So we'll have everything done by tomorrow at 10 a.m. Can you pick up your car then or will you come for it after work? Our sales department is open until 8."

The mechanic doesn't tell you that the total cost of the not-so-bad repair exceeds the blue book value of your car and that the sales guy left minding the shop after hours knows nothing about ringing up a repair using a credit card.

Sunny dentists deserve a special non-Novocaine-assisted spot in the ninth circle of Dante's Dental Inferno.

"OK, just a little more drilling to remove that rotten root and then we'll wash everything out and insert the rubber replacement liquid to take the place of the nerve. We'll glue a temporary cap on the tooth and you'll be all set until the permanent cap comes in next week."

All right, just another hour in the chair you think to yourself as you struggle with the plastic suction tubes in your mouth that have you ensnarled like a marlin off Key West. Then you have to come back next week and do it all over again.

Then there is the sunny guidance counselor who tries to be cheery about the whole college application process.

"Applying to this school isn't bad. Students just have to fill out the application, write the personal statement of purpose and compose an academic essay about the decline of heroes, and send in their SATs and achievement tests. Don't worry, the SAT is no longer as crucial an admissions indicator as it used to be, certainly not at this school.

"They look at other things like students' overall academic achievement records, their activities outside the classroom, leadership abilities, skills like having mastery of a classical musical instrument or having been published in a mainstream journal or performed the lead role in an off-Broadway play or played semi-pro baseball or performed retinal reattachment surgery, that sort of thing.

"Students just need to try to relax and smile occasionally. Possessing a sunny personality is important too."

So, OK. Let me try the sunny approach to this column. There, it is finished. All I have to do is perform a spellcheck, write a catchy headline, select a pull quote, lay it out on a dummy page, send it to pagination, get it back, proofread it and send it to press before deadline.

And, oh yes, after publication, take a few dozen angry calls from meteorologists, mechanics, dentists and guidance counselors. I'd rather retake the SAT, but I've misplaced my aptitude somewhere.

45.

THANKSGIVING:
GAMBITS AMONG THE GIBLETS

If you thought last Thanksgiving was difficult sitting next to crazy Uncle Ed, wait until this year. The nation is more polarized than it has been since the Vietnam War and making things worse is that your family has more factions than the Italian Parliament.

You will have to avoid talking about any political topic. The War in Iraq, stem cell research, faith-based initiatives, the Patriot Act, Condi, Colin, Rummy - all carry enough internal dynamite to blow up the Ted Williams Tunnel. That is, of course, if they get the 10,000 leaks fixed first, so the Back Bay water doesn't smother the fuse.

Forget about discussing alternative energy sources like wind power. Remember, cousin Dennis summers on Nantucket and raves about the view. You can't even talk about windsurfing. That's a Kerry sport, like duck hunting. Oh, let's not go there.

How about small talk about TV? Forgetaboutit. If you say you miss Speedle on "CSI-Miami," Emily Procter fans will say his leaving the show allows Emily/Calleigh Duquesne more space to develop her character. And don't choose a favorite player on "Survivor" or "Fear Factor." Too emotionally charged. By the way, how many permutations of Fear Factor are there? Fear Factor Twins, Fear Factor Couples, Fear Factor Friends, Fear Factor Bipolar Patients, Fear Factor Vegetarians, Fear Factor Civil War Buffs, Fear Factor Claustrophobes, Fear Factor Felons, Fear Factor Victoria Secret Models, Fear Factor Voyeurs, Fear Factor Psychiatrists.

Ever notice on "Antiques Roadshow" that people never have bought what they carry to the show, they "purchased" it. Purchase is one of those words people use when they want to appear proper and grammatical. "My aunt purchased this Van Gogh painting at a yard sale in Phoenix for $17." "My great-grandmother purchased this Tiffany vase in Paris when she attended the 1900 World's Fair." Just once I wished they would say: "I bought this painting from one of your appraisers in New York and now I'm told I spent $10,000 too much for it."

Praising the turkey is even frowned upon these days. Detailed discussions about the soporific effect of tryptophan could ignite a firestorm of comments about meat eating, sleep deprivation and worst nightmare of all, dieting. Atkins versus Slim Fast versus Jenny Craig versus South Beach versus WeightWatchers - these are topics more volatile than the gas used in the Hindenburg Airship.

What makes this all the worse is that you will be spending up-close-and-personal time with family you see only once a year and for good reason. It isn't so much that they live far away, but that they share similar genomic material with you and obey the magnetic law: like particles repel. All those like particles in the same room are enough to blow the walls out.

It is clear that the most successful strategy is to minimize the captive time at the table. If you constantly pop up to check something outside the room, then there are fewer chances you will become embroiled in some argument. Some gambits used by still-married couples are the following:

"I have to go out and check on my left front tire. It has a slow leak and I don't want to have to jack up the car to change it."

"I have to call the office. They're doing a network system update and I forgot to log off. Don't want to lose my files."

"I left my cell phone in the car."

"I forgot to tell the dog watcher where I left Gracie's food."

"I need to go out and get something from the drug store."

"I have to bring something in from the car."

"I have got to clean my glasses."

"I need to check on the score of my high school football game."

"I have to go help in the kitchen." (This one won't be believable.)

"I need to talk to Bob (or whoever is out of the room at the moment) about something."

"I am volunteering later today and need to call to make final arrangements."

"I have got to call the West Coast before they leave for their festivities."

"I don't feel well. I'll be right back."

This last works pretty well for me, especially when I leave clutching my chest.

Happy Thanksgiving.

46.

RIGHT TOOL FOR RIGHT JOB
— SOMEWHERE

Now that I have every tool I need, I can't find them.

My garage resembles a Grand Canyon of tools that I accrued over the decades and which now live in metallic strata around the garage. I am under orders to organize the garage, reclaim all usable space, liberate it from the clutter and return to base. I was on "recon" in the garage the other day and spied several tools of yesteryear.

In my collection is a long, offset faucet wrench with piranha jaws I used in 1986 to remove a sink faucet. I have a series of pipe wrenches that range from the merely mortal-sized to those wielded by steam fitters with Popeye biceps. I have taps and dies to repair the bolts I cross-threaded and ruined. I own a full set of SAE wrenches including crescent-moon shaped starter bolt wrenches I wielded to remove the starter motor on a 1969 Pontiac. I also own a full set of metric wrenches to use on post-1970 cars. I continue to be amazed that the most popular bolt on said cars is the 13mm. Tell me again why I have every other metric socket? All I need are a dozen or so 13mm ones.

I own the star-shaped Torx screwdrivers to remove those oddly shaped screws the car designers devilishly install in every modern headlight lens.

I have an array of tools but it is like sorting snowflakes. I have one toolbox with car tools, another with plumbing tools, yet another with a mixture of both. One toolbox is filled with lineman pliers, wire strippers, cable connectors, everything one would need to do heavy-duty electrical work. I have carpentry tools on one work bench. Drill bits and augers, along with my English-made brace set, reside in my carpenter's long box. Block planes and jack planes hang from the walls of my workshop or lie under the bench next to my router, I think.

Although I have a general idea of where things are, it really becomes a treasure hunt.

I stumble across tools I absolutely had to have in 1964 and they are next to things like a parallel printer head that I had re-soldered to make a dot matrix printer work. Remember dot matrix? They are the ones still used at the national car repair shops that print out your receipt in a six-foot-long scroll that the service manager folds on the perforated line and separates, folds and separates, again and again.

Last year, I bought a complete, carry-along tool kit that fit in a three-cantilever, hard-plastic box. After using it only once, I was unable to get the screwdrivers and drills back into their unforgivingly tight plastic slots. I stepped on the drills. I pounded on them with a ball peen hammer until the case dented. I tried wedging them into place. I needed the jaws of life to open up the slots to get the tools in. Not being a firefighter or auto body man, I don't have said jaws and my tools slide all over the tool case, fall out and eventually rest precariously under my vehicles' tires in the garage.

That is what happens with the tool kits I can find. The other tools and kits I can't find, not even with a Geiger counter. I know they are out there and that I used them on one particularly difficult project, but they are "in the wind" as they say on TV cop shows about suspects who have escaped.

My plan is to take my 100-pound-pull magnet and troll through the garage. Anything I collect I will put in a mound. Then, under the cover of darkness, I will roll in the multi-drawer toolbox on wheels that I hope to buy surreptitiously this weekend. You know the kind. They look like metal versions of Mayan temples with the series of ascending steps up the front. Then I will put all the wrenches in five of the drawers, all the sockets in other drawers, small hand tools in the hidden shelves below the drawers, and so on.

I will have everything in one space. Of course, I will have to keep my truck outside now, but I will know just where to find that 13mm socket wrench. It will be somewhere in drawer 37.

47.

SURVIVING A WORLD WITHOUT WORK

(Editor's note: As of this writing, there are 517 Westford residents who are listed as unemployed by the Massachusetts Division of Employment and Training. This figure does not include those unemployed who are no longer eligible to receive unemployment benefits or those who have dropped out of the work force.)

Bill (not his real name) is 53 years old and has been out of work as a technology manager for two years. He is tall and slim and his hair is slightly graying at the temples. He is physically active and carries himself with an air of a man on the go.

Even though he is unemployed, he gets up each morning, dresses in pressed slacks, a button-down dress shirt and polished shoes, and heads to a local diner where he has a cup of coffee and reads the morning paper. He appears to be just another busy manager en route to his job.

After his morning coffee, Bill heads over to the post office to buy some stamps. He tries to go somewhere different each morning and get something small, something that costs less than a dollar. He finds himself talking too much to cashiers and to people waiting in line with him and walking too slowly through the store. Working people run silent, run deep and run fast through their lives and have very little time for small talk.

After Bill's daily purchase, he drives home to his basement office where he proceeds to work the phone. He knows that important networking calls have to be made in that one-hour window from 8 a.m. to 9 a.m. No employed people want to talk to an out-of-work guy during the rush of the day - no matter how funny he is or how close they were to him when he was working. People have incredibly accurate radar and can detect when the person on the other end of the line is hunting for a job. They sense damage, an almost unspeakable feeling of walking death and they avoid the person like carrion.

Bill knows this from the quiet, serious tones he hears from people he calls. It's as if each person were a thoracic surgeon with a bad prognosis to deliver.

After 9 o'clock, the day yawns ahead of him. He spends a lot of time online looking at job listings, most of which are not in his field and which are just slightly above entry-level positions. On those extremely rare occasions when he gets a chance to talk to a hiring manager on the phone, he finds he must be more positive and perky than a recent college graduate.

He has removed any sense of time from his résumé and has trimmed his list of accomplishments so he looks less senior and less expensive. In his last interview, he didn't even ask what the salary was, a clear sign, he thought later, of how desperate he was to find a job.

Keeping up his spirits and feeling that he is still worth something are the twin challenges of his day. He dreads Thanksgiving and the upcoming holiday season. Everyone will ask how he's doing, what his prospects are, all the details. They think they are showing him signs of encouragement when actually Bill would really just like to sit and watch the Detroit Lions win the Thanksgiving Day football game. It is ironic that a working person is allowed undisturbed quiet on a holiday, and a non-working person is expected to field questions, suffer interrogations and generally account for himself.

There is also a sense from members of his wife's family that they wish Bill would do something, show some movement, as if he weren't doing anything at all to find a job. But he has. He has gone through the outplacement program provided by his former employer when he was laid off and all they said was to network, network, network. They claimed that most jobs worth having are never advertised and the only way to get one is to find someone who knows of one before the rest of unemployed America finds out.

But the job scene has changed because the jobs are gone. His colleagues who were also downsized have abandoned their fields, and even the towns they have lived in for the past two decades, and have opened bed and breakfasts in North Carolina or "retired." Bill wonders how they can retire with mortgages still unpaid, with no health benefits and with more than 10 years to go before qualifying for Social Security.

He takes solace in the fact that he has not given up and that he still manages to get an interview every three months. When that stops, he thinks he will stop. Then he will take any job that is available, including being a clerk at a retail store if he has to do so.

His wife has returned to work and is staying late each night and hopes to get more overtime. She seldom smiles anymore. She never asks about his day and never talks about hers. They have a marriage of convenience.

But Bill perseveres. He can still do the crossword puzzle faster than anyone in the family and walk up hills without puffing. He isn't dead yet. He hopes tomorrow he'll get an interview, and the tomorrow after that, land a job. He yearns to be in the workplace and meet someone at the coffee machine and talk about business. If he ever gets back, he promises himself never to be negative again.

That's the ticket. He will stay positive. People with futures are positive. Positive Bill, that's what he will be known as.

Now if he could only stay that way after 9 a.m.

48.

RUMINATIONS ON BEING THE MAN IN A VAN

I have a friend who is a Man in a Van.

He is an electrician who drives a rolling workshop filled with switches and sockets, cables and components. He can pull up to a house, diagnose a problem, go to his van for parts and tools and repair what's broken right on the spot.

I wish there were an equivalent for editors. I could see myself rolling up to someone's house with my van filled with verbs and subjunctives. Laptop booted up, cursor at the ready, I would be the embodiment of Dr. Rewrite making house calls.

Or much grander, imagine Stephen Hawking as the Man in the Van. I could envision him inside his white step-van parked outside the physics building at Cambridge University as he thought about black holes. From time to time he would reach into a canister filled with mathematical equations, extract one and put it in his tool belt. Imagine his invoice: Quantum equations, $175. Labor, $60,000.

Actually, the latter part is more in line with master plumbers than cosmologists.

Have you ever been able to get a plumber to do anything for under $100? I haven't. There is the weekend rate, the night rate, the Sunday double time rate and the holiday rate. Topping all of those rates is the emergency rate when the plumber promises to come within the half-hour. That costs big time, as Dick Cheney would say.

At the risk of getting swamped with angry e-mails from plumbers, let's forge ahead and do the math. I called the plumber three times last month. Each time he came on a Saturday and spent an hour on each of my three problems: a burst pipe under the sink, a faulty faucet in the bathroom that needed replacing, a leaking water filter that needed to be removed and re-installed. The costs were $300, $400 and $300. That's $1,000 for three hours of work. So, let's say he made $300 an hour. So, that's about $8,400 for a six-day week. (And I have built in traveling time in that figure.) So let's say he gets two weeks' vacation and works only 50 weeks. Well, 50 times $8,400 comes to $420,000 a year. Let's say that half that goes to materials and expenses. That leaves the plumber with an income of $210,00. Rather presidential, we think.

I am not begrudging paying people with skills and talent. Have you ever tried to sweat pipes that carry water under high pressure? How about installing a water heater? These tasks done badly can result in thousands of dollars of damage. So, it really is a pay me now or pay me later dilemma.

But let's get back to my Man in the Van editor fantasy. My invoice would total as follows: verbs, $37; metaphor, $14; memorable phrase that will eventually end up on a bumper sticker, $28; labor $25.

So whether I am commissioned to write a Gettysburg Address or simply edit down the steamy diary of a plumber, I will earn each year about three days' worth of plumbing income.

I can take that to the bank. In my van.

49.

TO HAVE AND TO HOLD, EVERY 3,000 MILES

Traditional marriage vows include the words: to have and to hold, in sickness and in health, for richer or poorer. If you are a heterosexual man who grew up when "Bonanza" was the most-popular show on television, the vows also contain two additional conjugal conditions: (1) The husband will uncomplainingly take out the garbage; and (2) he will get the oil in the car changed.

Let's talk about the latter. ("Yet again with the oil thing?" I can hear my wife saying as I write this. "This is your idea of a Valentine column, is it?" she asks, always rhetorically.)

As a do-it-yourselfer, I always took pride on being able to save money by changing the oil in my vehicle's engine myself. I succeeded at that grimy task for years. I acquired a whole garage full of tools: oil filter wrenches, some that fit snugly over the oil filter and were turned by a ratchet; others that clamped onto the oil filter to help twist it off. Some of the tools even worked. Not the clamping ones, however, They usually slipped, or worse, crushed the oil filter causing it to split and leak oil on the concrete garage floor I had just washed.

The oil removal operation also involved jacks and jack stands but these eventually proved too cumbersome and too life-threatening. One always wondered what would happen if the jack stand tipped over while one was underneath the car trying to twist off an oil filter that had fused on from the heat of a nearly nuclear summer.

I eventually graduated to car ramps. These were two steel ramps on which you drove the front wheels of the car. They had a slight lip on the end that provided a little bump when you hit it that indicated you needed to come to a full stop or risk going over the edge. I rolled over that lip once with a front-wheel-drive car and found myself hung up on the ramps with the front wheels spinning in the air like a scene from the movie, "Earthquake." I had to get two floor jacks and jack the car up and move the ramps in position and then let the car down with a thump that could be heard (I was told) even over the booming baritone of Victor Kiriakis on "Days of Our Lives" in the living room.

Needless to say, I am more careful now and often ask my marriage partner to stand on the side of the garage and yell when I have driven the car fully on the ramps. This is not her favorite thing to do. The phrase, "Stop, you idiot," has reverberated more than once in my not-so-quiet garage.

Now an undesirable feature of these steel ramps is that its edges are sharp, sharper than King Arthur's fabled sword, Excalibur. Well, one summer day, without thinking (not unusual for me, I am told), I placed the ramps, not inside the garage on the impenetrable concrete floor, but outside in the beautifully warm weather on the asphalt driveway. I drove my car onto the ramps without incident and experienced one of those rare Zen moments when the oil filter spun off effortlessly, the oil flow landed precisely in the center of the catch basin I was using. Installing a new filter and adding fresh oil went as smoothly as a David Copperfield illusion.

It wasn't until I rolled the heavy V8-equipped, four-door sedan off the ramps that I noticed that the ramp edges had sliced about two inches deep into the asphalt. I put on some work gloves to protect my hands from the keen ramp edges, and with a deadlift that an Olympic power lifter would admire, rescued the ramps from what had become the LaBrea tar pit formerly known as my driveway.

Needless to say, I was crestfallen. In fact, more than my crest would have fallen had I not rushed over to the home center and bought 10 pounds of asphalt to repair the damage. I filled the slices with the asphalt mix and used the same steamroller car to tamp down the asphalt into a seamless black blanket. Of course, my wife, the inspector general from battalion headquarters, did comment on how I now had created an asphalt quilt that looked like something one might see on the Central Artery during the height — make that depth — of the Big Dig. "You, idiot."

Soon, I joined the Technology Revolution and bought a gadget that consisted of a large one-gallon tank into which an air pump was hermetically sealed. All one had to do was to pump out the air from the enclosed tank and create a vacuum. Then you stuck a plastic transparent tube down the oil filler pipe and sucked out the oil into the gulping tank. No muss, no fuss. Well, the vacuum I managed to create would suck out about 12 ounces of oil and then stop. The tube would drip oil upon removal and squirt this way and that like a skit involving a fire hose on the loose from an "I Love Lucy" show.

Last year, for Christmas, I bought myself an oil pump that allegedly works from the battery of the car's engine and pumps the oil out into a waiting container. I have not as yet had the courage to try it. I am, however, content to think of it working.

The last few months I have been going to those fast oil change franchise places where they try to sell you new air filters, new wipers, new gas line filters and other gadgets that actually need replacing only once every geologic era. I say no to all those attempts and just ask for the oil change. They frown.

I wait in the waiting room as they pump oil down the crankcase, start up the engine and do a cursory check of the transmission fluid. And, then, instead of having done the job myself for only $12, I fork over $32 to them. Sometimes, I have to retighten the oil filter because they don't tighten it quite enough. They never ever replace the washer on the oil drain plug as they should once a year. Instead they look at me when I inquire about it as if I were Dr. Frankenstein asking where I could get a good, healthy brain that no one is using at the moment. Certainly not at this oil change facility, I think to myself.

To complicate matters, on those rare balmy days when I do indeed change the oil myself, I must run the gauntlet at the municipal recycling center. Waste oil must be in leak-proof plastic gallon jugs. They must be placed in the oil container shed on shelves two feet off the ground and be handled with the care of a haz-mat team at Three Mile Island.

So, I find myself more and more at the fast lube places watching reruns in the waiting room and returning every 3,000 miles or three months, whichever comes first.

What choice do I have? I made a vow.

50.

ON SPRING AND A WEIGHTY WHARF

The temperature is way below freezing as I write this, but calendrically (now there's an adverb), spring is officially less than a week away. Spring is a time when a lot of people think about getting their garden tools sharpened, their lawn mowers tuned, their boats' hulls scraped, and their baseball gloves oiled.

I'm thinking about how heavy everything has become this spring. It is as if I fell asleep and awoke somewhere else on the Periodic Chart of the Elements. Take the wharf I have at the lake, for example. For years I have thought nothing of putting on some bathing trunks, stepping into the cold lake water in the spring and man-hauling the 8-foot-long wooden wharf into the water. In the past, I was usually able, with a few accompanying Cro-Magnon grunts, to lift one side of the wharf with one hand while placing a stake under it. Then I would repeat the process on the other side and then nail both stake legs in place. For some strange reason having nothing to do with the wharf itself, it has become as heavy as if it were made from solid uranium.

I use the wharf primarily as a place from which I cast psychedelically colored lures into the water at snobbish bass. I also use it as a tie point for my kayak and small fishing boat. The wharf extends my reach into the lake just enough to allow me to be a fisherman, kayaker and swimmer.

That is why I am so intent on getting the wharf in this year without getting help. It's a male thing, I guess, like changing a tire. So, I have a plan. I am going to take the whole structure apart. Devilishly clever, you say? Yes, my plan is to turn the wharf upside down and nail two one-inch-wide fir strips on the backs of the boards that serve as the wharf's decking. I will nail the strips so they form two 4-foot sections. Then I will flip the wharf right side up (a lot of flipping here for someone of my vintage, don't you think?) and remove the nails that hold the deck boards to the rails. The end result is I will have three lighter parts to deal with instead of one very heavy beast.

I will take the bare frame, which will look like a giant rectangle made by a mad, hammer-wielding Euclidean, out into the water and affix it to stakes. Then I will carry one section of deck out and lay it on the frame, then the other. Then I will take just a few nails and tack the deck plates into place. And, voila, a wharf that even an empty-nester can maneuver by himself. In the fall, I will reverse the process.

Of course, this new configuration will mean that I will have to store three wharf parts instead of one. This will be a problem. I will have to lash the pieces together or they may find themselves convenient firewood for next winter's ice fishermen. But that is not too much to pay to be able to have a one-man wharf.

Once the wharf is in place, I will still need to find a way to get my 10-foot-long, 4-foot-wide boat down a flight of concrete stairs to the water. I have an array of moving and appliance dollies, some with hard wheels, others with pneumatic wheels. One of these devices might work to help transport the boat down the stairs. The problem is the width of the boat. It won't fit width-wise through the opening between the two stone walls that stand like gun emplacements looming over the water.

I will have to stand the boat on end and somehow wheel it down the stairs pausing one step before the wall opening. Then, I will perform a Fred Astair dance step and swivel my boat partner 90 degrees and glide it through the opening. Of course, what I have to prevent from happening is having the boat teeter out of control and crash into my little wharf, smashing it and the boat to Humpty-Dumpty smithereens.

I usually rely on ratchet straps to hold things on to the dolly. I learned long ago that ropes and knots loosen after descending two stairs. I tighten the ratchet tie-downs until strumming them produces a musical note somewhere near middle C. Then, I know the object is securely fastened. Of course, unloosening the ratchet lock to get the object off can bruise a thumb from time to time, so I will use a pair of pliers or a screwdriver this year.

So, that's my spring launch plan, the warp and woof of my wharf.

You know, come to think of it, I may have someone help me this year. I just won't tell anyone about it.

51.

IT'S OK TO BE WICKED SMART

You are what you read. You are also what you say and how you say it. Using appropriate language often determines whether you succeed in society and is almost as important as having professional skills and knowledge. There are many examples from history.

Abraham Lincoln's oratory set the trajectory of his success from an early age and helped propel him over some of the most difficult political obstacles ever faced by a US president. ("The ballot is stronger than the bullet." Perhaps his most famous utterance is: " ... government of the people, by the people, for the people, shall not perish from the earth.")

Winston Churchill rallied besieged Londoners with his speeches - "Never in the field of human conflict was so much owed by so many to so few" and "I have nothing to offer but blood, toil, tears and sweat." John F. Kennedy's "Ask not what your country can do for you; ask what you can do for your country" speech set the tone for a decade of volunteerism.

The above examples are, admittedly, fairly lofty. Nevertheless, even in our less-stratospheric, quotidian lives one finds examples of people who speak well and who try to communicate with others with some thoughtfulness. For them, language is not an anything-goes, disposable activity like dashing off an e-mail to the shipping department at Land's End.

Rather, language has weight and worth. It can persuade and sway. There are other benefits as well. Using the appropriate word and framing your thoughts with clarity are rewards in and of themselves. From rap to bumper stickers, from one-liners to doctoral dissertations, a well-wrought phrase can be just plain beautiful. Calling the Aegean a wine dark sea is one such example.

But there are those who think there is something pedantic or effete about using language that is literary. In schools, the kid who excels at Latin is often the same kid who is discriminated against by those who don't know a declension from a doughnut.

Gender discrimination against bookish people also abounds. Women who are intellectuals are often labeled as too masculine; men who are intellectuals are termed too feminine. Why is that?

People who are uneasy when they hear language with which they are unfamiliar often emit a hot plasma of defensiveness. Then there are those who dislike anything cerebral. Americans have a history of anti-intellectualism and are the very people who coined words like egghead and nerd to describe well-read or scientific people.

What a shame. Our language, with many contributions from Latin, Greek and William Shakespeare (the bard is credited with creating more than 1,500 words that are now commonplace in the English language) is rich with borrowings and adaptations. I like the commonly used word, postal, which has come to mean someone who goes berserk, which is derived from the abnormally high number of violent episodes by postal workers.

I also like the more abstruse phrase, Parthian shot, which has morphed into the current phrase, parting shot. The Parthians, enemies of ancient Rome, were known for their unusual tactics of feigning retreat. As they galloped away, they would suddenly swivel around on their horses and let fly an arrow at their unsuspecting enemy who had, to their dismay, lowered their weapons. This battle technique became known as the Parthian shot or parting shot.

So, here is my Parthian shot. In today's digital domain of "killer-ap" videos and disposable thoughts, the word may often be ignored. That is unfortunate. Nothing captures the imagination like an image that one can draw for oneself based on well-crafted text.

And if that text comes from someone who is well-educated and well-spoken, so be it. Don't apologize for your educational background and don't let people pigeon hole you or write you off just because they are insecure about their own abilities.

If they choose to go postal and try to give you an unwarranted Parthian shot, may they find themselves adrift on a wine dark sea - without a sextant, trigonometric tables or a copy of Homer.

52.

'Work deco' adorns cubicles

People decorate their work "stations" (we're moving away from the claustrophobia-inducing word cubicle) with pictures of their families, their significant others, their cats and dogs, horses and birds. They adorn their eight-hours-a-day areas with posters from theater events they have attended, with stuffed animals, with snapshots of their vacations in blue lagoons and with all manners of personal things to make bold visual statements that they have lives outside the office, or at least dreams of one.

I think it would be fun to bring into my sterile, insurance-office-look-alike work area my antique typewriter, a 1934 Royal portable, to indicate to visitors that this is indeed a newsroom. I got the typewriter years ago to add to my collection along with a classic Graflex Speed Graphic camera. That was the press photographer's main camera during the 1930s. It was the camera used by all those guys in gray suits who stuck their press passes in the hat bands of their fedoras and ran into locker rooms and called a boxer "champ," and a baseball player "slugger." You can see them in old movies like Ben Hecht's "Front Page" or "His Gal, Friday." That was also the time when if you were a reporter on a story, you could call the paper on one of those candlestick phones and yell, "Get me rewrite."

But if I were to bring in my old typewriter, I'm sure the editor who sits next to me would think nothing of grabbing a piece of yellow copy paper, inserting it in the typewriter and pounding out a story that would "bust this town wide open, Chief." He's that kind of guy.

So my work area is virtually unadorned, just one poster from a play at the local high school and a picture of a Westford town official. The picture is placed strategically at shoulder level so it has a clear sight line to my computer screen. It maintains an unblinking vigil making sure my copy is accurate. (The town official is an exacting individual and was the first person, actually the only person, to tell me that the Abbot School in Westford is spelled with just one "t." I thank the official for that spelling tip and for reminding me that, to a lot of people, getting things right is still important in the newspaper biz.)

But I wished I had more room to display nontraditional things. I think it would be a hoot to bring in a deep-sea diving suit, complete with massive brass diving bell head piece — the kind with screw threads on the collar. I would like to prop that up in the corner of my area and see what comments that would elicit. Or, alternatively, I think it would be fun to display a guillotine, circa early French Revolution, scaled down, of course, but I suspect there may be some OSHA rule prohibiting its display for safety reasons.

Or maybe I could ask to have one of those mahogany propeller ceiling fans installed above my computer like the ones you see in Rick's Place in "Casablanca." Or how about a mock-up of the bridge of the Starship "USS Enterprise," complete with blinking computer lights (my computer has pnly one light). It would also sport a chrome rail so Lt. Uhura and Mr. Spock won't topple off the communications/science deck and fall into Captain Kirk during those bumpy rides through a discontinuity in the space-time continuum? Too nerdy, you say.

OK, I guess I'll just have to risk it and bring in the old typewriter and hope that my work area visitors, who undoubtedly will not be able to resist the temptation to push down the keys, don't jam the ribbon.

53.

RETURN TO SENDER:
BRAGGING HOLIDAY CARDS

This is the time when we receive Christmas and holiday cards. Most of them are uplifting and generate warm feelings. But there is one type of year-end communication that irks me - the résumé-like note that regales the reader with the Olympian accomplishments of the sender's family during the past year.

Here is a typical sample.

"Lydia had a very busy year, what with delivering her fourth child, a bouncing baby boy, Thomas, and then being chosen to present the Karl Jung memorial lectures in psychiatry at the International Psychiatry Association in Geneva. Her husband, Charles, continues to be very busy as Deputy Director of the FBI but still finds time to be home for the major holidays. Jason loves Yale, and despite the vagaries of the MetroNorth commuter rail line, is enjoying traveling to New York for his master classes at Julliard. Mary loves being a grandmother for the fourth time and is back from her 23-city book-signing tour. She is absolutely thrilled that Larry McMurtry and his wife have decided to do the screenplay and that Steven Spielberg will direct. I find I am more busy in retirement than when I was running OmniGrowth. I had a few scary moments dealing with rogue waves in my run to Bermuda this spring but I am determined to win the Atlantic solo race this year in the post-55 category. I'm still doing a little consulting and spent last month in Riyadh. Well, that's all for now. Merry Christmas and Happy Holidays. "

Just for once I would appreciate receiving a less-glowing, more-honest family summary. Here is an example from the other end of the spectrum:

"It has been a very challenging year for the family. Emily gained 42 pounds while she was away at school and was dropped from the ski team. She didn't get into law school so has decided to spend the year working in retail in Brockton. Robbie has only two more months left on his sentence and is looking forward to coming home. Mary is lucky to have survived the layoffs at work but is worried about making it through the winter. I'm still looking for employment in my field but the so-called recovery hasn't generated any possibilities for me as yet. Howard, our golden retriever, continues to be the joy of our lives and is always there for us, no matter what. So, here's wishing you a Merry Christmas and what we hope will be a more prosperous New Year for all of us."

But, seriously, the holidays should be more about listening and accepting and helping and less about strutting. Being kind is still the greatest gift one can give this season.

Merry Christmas and Happy Holidays.

54.

YOUNG AND OLD:
MP3 VERSUS TIMEX

I think people would lead richer more rewarding lives if younger people thought more about the past and older people thought more about the future.

As an older person I can give you many details from every decade of my life. And yet, I have no idea what new developments and trends loom just over the horizon. I'm not even that knowledgeable about the present and things that are already here. For example, people of my generation may have heard of MP3 players but no one has actually seen one.

When someone young says Napster, we older folks hear NAFTA - the North American Free Trade Agreement - made famous for the sucking sound predicted by its opponent, presidential candidate Ross Perot, as US jobs were whooshed to Mexico, and arguably, lost forever.

Younger people have telescoped time. They define something really old as something that happened before Britney Spears kissed Madonna. Everything before then is mixed together: the Civil War, D-Day, juke boxes, Frank Sinatra, Thomas Edison, Eleanor Roosevelt — all turn and tumble in a kaleidoscope of undifferentiated history.

But who can blame them? We live in a disposable era in which things are designed to wear out and be replaced. My generation was the Timex generation where watches "took a licking but kept on ticking." Then, society emphasized quality and producing goods that last.

My favorite Timex commercial was the one in which Timex spokesman, newsman John Cameron Swayze, attached a Timex to one of the blades of a propeller on an outboard motor and then ran the motor at speed in the water. He would then stop the motor, tilt it up to the transom of the boat, remove the watch and show its face to the camera. The second hand of the watch pulsated around the dial every second proving that it was "still ticking."

Today, we wouldn't bother to undo the watch on the propeller; we would simply pull into a shore-side convenience store and buy a plastic digital watch for less than the price of a bottle of water.

We know that sooner or later everything will have a computer chip built into it. With nanotechnology, we can expect a revolution in the miniaturization of our computers and associated devices. Like the cell phone, which almost every teen-ager now owns, technology will continue to vault ahead and those quantum leaps will transform society.

What does it mean to have instant access to everyone everywhere? Will talk be so cheap and disposable that no one will say anything that cannot be compressed into a few words that can flash under a picture on a picture-phone?

Who will have the time to read something long like a book when the phone keeps ringing all day long with two- and three-word, "what's-up" messages? What implications does living in the digital present have for our lives? Is history important? If valuing history is generational, as I am strongly implying, then what should we do to have all of us, young and old, while looking forward, still be able to put things in historical context so as not to repeat our blunders?

I guess one could argue that the best of both worlds would be to augment our thought and lives with technology. I'm for that. I love to see and hear the actual video footage of Neil Armstrong as he stepped foot on the moon in 1969 - his footprint in the baking-powder moon dust, the sound of his voice being radioed over space with that characteristic time delay that indicates out-of-this-world distance. But I would also want to read a detailed account of the history of the Apollo Program and why the Cold War made the race to the moon possible, even vital, to the future of the super-powers.

So, herein lies a resolution. As an old guy, I will promise to access an online Web 'zine about technology and listen to some techno music on an MP3 player. In trade, I would urge a young person to read the first two chapters of Theodore White's brilliant book, "The Making of the President, 1960," to get some perspective on how presidential campaigns are waged and won.

If that fails to bring us common ground, then I suggest we head to Fenway and watch the Red Sox break our hearts: Young and old.

55.

THE WEATHER:
RAIN, RAW, RIDICULOUS

I don't like weathermen who take credit for sunny days but assume no responsibility for rainy days. Yes, I know I said weathermen, but it is usually the male meteorologist whose ego extends beyond the very troposphere. "I'm happy to bring you some bright sun, a blue sky, just a terrific day," I remember one weatherman proudly say last summer. Who does this guy think he is — Zeus?

Not this spring, however. The weather these days resembles the perpetual acid rain in the 1982 movie, "Blade Runner." Think Seattle relocated to the planet Pluto - gray skies, drizzle, refrigerator temperatures. People's moods are down to submarine levels where only whales are happy.

Weather forecasters are blaming a tantrum of the jet stream for the persistence of the vile weather. They now describe weather patterns in terms of weeks, not days. "This pattern looks like it will last well into next week." They might as well say, "This pattern will last well into the fall."

I remember years ago when the weatherman was a neat guy with cool toys. People then were not very sophisticated scientifically. In fact, many viewers in the early TV audience in the 1950s thought a meteorologist was a guy who studied rocks falling from space. I used to love to watch the weatherman as he described how a barometer worked and told us that air had weight and that if you monitored changes in the air pressure with a barometer you could predict the weather 12 to 24 hours in advance with a reliability of 85 percent.

That was before computer models, satellites and automated weather stations. Now, many average homes have digital weather stations that measure temperature, humidity, wind speed and direction, air pressure, rainfall, all instantly and on one plasma screen. But to give the forecasting technology its due, predicting the weather has become more precise, and with gigawatt Doppler radar, up close and personal. Nevertheless, viewers give forecasters bad grades because they tend to remember only those relatively rare times when the forecasters miscalculated the force of a coastal snow storm or the few times when they overestimated the snowfall. Actually, the accuracy of forecasts has risen over the years. (Astonishing when you reflect upon it, the devastating 1938 hurricane was a largely unpredicted event.)

But the increase in accuracy doesn't mean that the forecasters can take credit for the actual weather as if they turned a dial and made the clouds go away. Some viewers also resent the chirpy delivery of the weather forecaster who puts on a bright face and a sunny personality to distract from the endless icons of clouds and raindrops rolling across the seven-day forecast graphic. I do admire, however, the weather people's ability to point at symbols and cities on the map when what is really behind them is a blank green screen. The images are added electronically and the forecaster has to look at the actual broadcast image on a nearby monitor to see where his or her hands are pointing. It is like trying to grab a fish in a pond. The light bends and refracts and one usually misses snatching the fish by half a foot.

But at this point in our spring-as-nuclear-winter season, I would overlook the perky weatherman and his boasts of bringing us a perfect day. Dial away the gray, Mr. Weatherman, and bring us some sun.

56.

OF LEAVES, RAKES AND CHIROPRACTORS

The indigenous population of Massachusetts did not rake leaves. Well, not all the time the way we do in fall. Native peoples let the leaves fall where they may and went on about their lives without suffering painful blisters, wrenched backs or sore necks.

Fall has to be the best season for chiropractors. (An aside: did you know the noun for the activity the chiropractors practice is chiropractic, as in, "Dr. Jones studied chiropractic at the University of Such-and-Such." Sounds strange, doesn't it, using what appears to be an adjective as a noun? I would recommend some manipulating of the verbal vertebrae here.)

I have tried most of the methods of leaf collection. I have used hand-carried leaf blowers. These are effective when blowing leaves from flower beds or off one's driveway but not very practical on lawns that have a full carpet of wet maple leaves whose points seem snagged in the long grass you neglected to cut in the fall. The gas-powered hand-carried leaf blowers usually gum up after a season and you spend a great deal of time pulling the starter cord and uttering phrases you hear soldiers say during battle. The electric-powered leaf blowers are great if you can link two 100-foot cords together and pull the resultant serpent around corners of your house. The worst is when the cord becomes wedged underneath a tire on your car. Then you have to go over and free the cord and try to pay out as much cord as you can without it getting ensnarled on itself in some form of a Gordian knot that takes an entire afternoon to untangle.

I have also used the gas-powered leaf blowers on wheels. Of course, not having the finances of Bill Gates, I bought a leaf blower that has a fixed air discharge chute so you have to push the blower in one direction and pull it back in the other. This push-pull approach causes some wavy lines because you cannot see where you are pulling the machine because you have to watch where you are going when you are pulling.

Then, of course, you find that a five horsepower unit, which the salesman had told me was powerful enough for "every home job," is not powerful enough for even 10 percent of the home jobs. It is adequate for small, dry leaves on Teflon surfaces but inadequate for layers of leaves on grass. For this, I would presume you would need something on the order of Pratt & Whitney's JT9D, the jet engine that delivers 46,300 pounds of thrust and is used to power the 747. In any case, your five horsepower unit can blow leaves until they get about six inches high and then they just clump together and play dead.

So out come the rakes. I have tried wire-tined rakes, plastic-fingered rakes and rakes with wooden tines that look as if they came from the Plimouth Plantation. They all work pretty well for the first half hour and then you begin to notice that your wrist hurts and your fingers seem to have gone into a spasm. You walk around the yard like some skeletal monster from the crypt on Halloween - which is when you should have done the leaves in the first place.

Once you get the leaves together, then you have to dispose of them. This can mean scooping up 10,000 handfuls and placing them in plastic leaf bags. This requires the services of an accomplice to keep the mouth of the bag open while you are depositing the leaves into the bag. Or you can use an aluminum trash barrel and fill that up a few thousand times. If it isn't too windy you can try throwing a plastic tarp on the lawn and raking a pile of leaves onto it and then dragging the tarp to the end of your property and dumping the leaves down the banking and hope your neighbor isn't watching. (This is what I do, by the way.)

My neighbors don't do anything as plebian as rake their own leaves. They hire teams of Ghostbusters who come in with blowers on their backs. They blow the leaves into the road and amass them into a gargantuan pile. Then they vacuum them into a truck that looks like a Conestoga wagon and then they haul the leaves away.

I marvel at this from afar as I try to walk through ankle-deep, pointy oak leaves that exhibit better staying power than the Patriots' defense. But there is no rest from the weekend war. Leaves keep falling and carpeting the lawn and it seems endless. Eventually all the leaves fall, the tarp is dragged for the 161st time and you are done.

All that is left is to go to the good doctor who studied chiropractic at the local college, and who friends say, could make the Tin Man from the Wizard of Oz dance.

57.

TAKING STOCK AFTER THE HOLIDAY

   The days immediately after Labor Day find kids back at school and adults back from vacations. We return to reality.
   I am not going back without a fight. On Labor Day, I floated lazily in a canoe behind a lake's lone island. I floated among the lily pads, fishing rod in hand, just as I have done all summer. I had already that day caught some good-sized blue gills who fought me like Sugar Ray in the clinches. They seemed tireless. Large-mouth bass, however, when hooked "sound" like whales and dive deep into the weeds hoping to dislodge the hook. Then, rather quickly, the bass stop their descent as they try to lull us into letting the line go slack so they can jump off the hook when you don't expect it. These big guys are wily. The blue gills don't think; they pull and fight even when they are out of the water.
   As I was considering the fighting tactics of both species, I felt a cool wind blow in quietly from the northwest, right out of Canada and right into my face. It was a subtle but unmistakable sign of fall. Soon we will hear geese honking south and watch leaves fall into the water on the edge of the lake and drift, green on blue, until they get water-logged and sink to the bottom.
   A woodpecker pounds on an old oak on the shore and the rapidity of his rapping is startling. It is so fast it is almost pneumatic. How does he do it for so long without his head and beak hurting?
   On the hill away from the water it seems almost calm but here at the end of a long fetch on the lake the wind has stirred up a chop that makes paddling difficult. I have to get off the stern seat and kneel on the canoe bottom to stabilize the craft and to keep the bow from tossing to-and-fro in the gusts.
   It is tough going. A mile seems like a crossing of the North Atlantic. My shoulders ache but I am going at speed now, nearly planing off, heading directly into the wind and slicing through the chop, my cabin in sight beneath tall pines. The wind is so strong I will have to shoot past the landing and drift into shore. The most dangerous time will be when I am abeam the wind and the waves. I am glad I am wearing a

life vest, although it makes for cumbersome Michelin-man paddling.

I drive the bow clockwise as I pass the desired landing spot and the canoe moves rapidly sideward. This will not be a landfall I hoped someone would capture on film. The bottom scrapes on the sand and I miraculously avoid some rather large boulders as the canoe grinds to a stop. The wind is whistling now as the leading edge of a cold front marches across the lake. The waves lap the sides of the beached canoe with loud thwarps.

Soon I will have unloaded my gear and hauled the canoe up the banking, perhaps for the last time until spring. At the top of the banking I stop and sit on the canoe and look out at the lake. The sun is setting and shafts of light sparkle on the western waters.

I think it is a good thing to notice the passing of seasons. It is indeed true they move more quickly the older we are. In our 20s they seemed sluggish; now they rush by like scenes glimpsed through a railway car window in an old 1940s movie. Perhaps in our dotage, they all will be just a blur. That is why, the post-Labor Day time period is such a good opportunity for personal stock-taking..

Where are we headed? How far have we gone? Are we still on course? Good things to ask ourselves after another Labor Day but before the inevitable blur.

58.

April,
and Cruel Blades of Grass

Poet T.S. Eliot is right: April is the cruelest month. Not because it breeds "lilacs out of the dead land," but because of yard work.

Now I admit that I equate yard work with prison yards: It is that place where you are forced to exercise for a given period every day and you are never done until it snows and the yard is closed. There is also another similarity, and that is my yard - alias, my lawn - has the same trampled look as many yards at penitentiaries. Blame it on the nocturnal wildlife.

My lawn sports several rectangular areas that look as if someone has randomly turned over the turf with a jack hammer. I telephoned the town animal control officer to inquire what kind of animal was churning through my lawn and she said "skunks." Skunks? "Yes, skunks." It seems they like to eat the grubs that lie beneath the lawn in spring.

Well, one early pre-dawn morning a few days after the call to the animal control officer, I went out to retrieve the newspaper. It is "delivered" by a man, who identifies himself only as Sergei. Sergei drives a white station wagon with one brown door on the driver's side and throws the paper out his window. You can hear the newspaper hit the pavement followed by the sound of rubber squealing as the car speeds off into the pre-dawn blackness. You can hear the car's blown muffler bellowing for blocks.

After picking up the newspaper at the end of my driveway this dark morning, I walked back to the house and spied something on the lawn so huge it could have appeared in the ring on World Wrestling Entertainment's "SmackDown." It was a skunk. It was so big, it waddled. When it saw me it paraded nonchalantly over my lawn and into the woods.

So this was the nocturnal lawn destroyer, eh? Well, let's hope there are enough grubs for him or the asphalt shingles will be next, I said out loud, maintaining my reputation in the neighborhood as the strange guy who is up when he should be asleep and asleep when he should be up and who talks to himself.

The next day I decided to surf the Internet and find out how to deal with skunks. All the remedies carried so many cautionary warnings that I quickly determined it was easier to dispose plutonium than it was to risk exposure to the devastating spray from a skunk. Luckily, the skunk issue was really not the problem.

A couple of days later, just after leaving for work, I remembered I had left my sunglasses on the kitchen table. So I turned my car around and drove back into the driveway and there were three crows happily drilling through the topsoil of my lawn retrieving worms and grubs. They were having a wonderful time.

I got out of my car and stamped my foot on the sidewalk. I don't know whether crows smile or not, but I think they merely smiled at me and kept on excavating my lawn in search of the mother of all grubs.

This would not do. I immediately went to my lawn and garden shop and came home with chemical sprays that are supposed to help kill grubs and also make the grass unpalatable to birds. Well, the crows treated the chemicals like salad dressing and continued to peck through the lawn until all the grubs were gone. They then flew over a few houses away and started to work on the unkempt lawn of a neighbor whose yard work expertise makes me look like the host of PBS' "Victory Garden."

Well, anyway, once the crows left, I was able to start the annual spring yard cleanup and preparation work. The lawn in the back of my house is shaded by two towering oak trees that provide lovely shade during July but which drop branches and twigs throughout the winter. These branches seem to have woven themselves into a kind of wooden trampoline. When I would pick up one branch, a hundred other ensnarled branches would vibrate like a giant arboreal net. Gosh, what would happen if the tyrannosaurus skunk were to get trapped in this wooden web? The property would be uninhabitable for months, I said aloud once again.

I couldn't worry about that now because I had hours of back-breaking pick-up-sticks work to do. After a few Saturdays of clean up, it was finally time to put lime down on the lawn. This process, I am told, is a sure sign that the lawn owner doesn't know what he or she is doing. Experts say most fertilizing and conditioning work is done in the fall. Springtime is when you do a little spreading of chemicals to prevent things like grubs from infecting your lawn.

Anyway, lime spreading is kind of fun. You can throw this white powder everywhere, get your shoes covered with the stuff, as well as ruin a good pair of jeans. But there is something very primordial about throwing lime around. It just feels right even though it is wrong.

Well, amazingly, in a few weeks, my lawn will have recovered from the Hitchcock crows and my lime treatments and there will be grass to be mowed. I am one of the few people in the neighborhood who does not have a riding lawn mower, tractor or lawn service. I simply pull the cord on my lawnmower, hope it starts, and walk behind it, row after row after row until it runs out of gas.

I have often thought that I have reached the age when I should be piloting one of those fancy zero-radius riding mowers. I could wear the baseball cap that guys my age wear, keep a can of soda in the soda holder on the right fender and wear a short-sleeved shirt buttoned all the way up. Ever notice that old guys not only drive with their left directional signals permanently on but also button the top button on their sports shirts? Well, that will be me, perhaps next year. Skunk and crows not withstanding, I will be all buttoned up with no place to go but my yard.

59.

UNDERSTANDING NUANCES OF SNOW BLOWER ETIQUETTE

I need to bring up a controversial subject that I have postponed writing about for years. No, it's not the decline of the Republic, but snow blower etiquette.

I live in the suburbs and my two-car-wide driveway shares a side street with two neighbors. The street is not plowed by the town but by a private contractor employed by my neighbors. I don't use the services of the plow guy because I have a honkin' big-block snow thrower with six speeds forward, two reverse and a discharge plume that can reach 60 feet in height, if the snow is powdery. With the appropriate lighting, the snow spray can be made to look like Old Faithful at Yellowstone.

Therein lies the ethical dilemma. If I am clearing the shared street before the plow guy arrives, can I deposit half the snow on my neighbor's lawn? I am sheepish about this. Usually I secretly direct the plume into the trees behind my neighbor's house but not on his open lawn where he can see me. This is not easy to get away with because he is at the window more than Norman Bates in Hitchcock's "Psycho."

Often his hired guy doesn't come to plow until the next day, or until he has finished with his commercial clients, whichever comes later. So this means that the shared road remains snow-laden until I clear it. In a particularly snowy season, I run out of room to deposit the snow from the street and need to put some of it elsewhere - like on my neighbor's land.

I guess I could have what the U.S. State Department calls a "full and frank" discussion with my neighbor and work out snow deposit rights. I am reluctant to do that because this is the same neighbor who practices a policy of reverse eminent domain and believes that all municipally owned land within walking distance of his lot lines is his property. He has developed play areas, rail fences, an ice skating rink - even a scenic overlook - on wilderness town land that just happens to be next to his.

If he were to star in a Louis L'Amour western, he would be the cattleman who tears down barbed wire fences and shoots his six gun at sod busters. It is ironic that this is the same guy who protects his own property like the Russians guard their air space.

I have tried like some mad mathematician to throw the snow in discrete squares - this square will be placed next to my fence, this one will be shot behind the rhododendron, this one will be deposited near the bird house. But maybe it is that enforced precision that inspires me to shoot a plume into my neighbors trees with downright abandon.

There is something existentially freeing to blast snow above the rooftops and watch the resultant clouds crash against second-floor windows in mini-blizzards.

Here's a solution. I'll do more of the snow blowing at night, late at night, say just as "CSI-Miami" is coming on TV. That way when Horatio puts on his shades and looks into the Miami sun, no one will realize that a wild man is outside blowing snow where owls fear to tread.

60.

CO MONITOR INSTALLATION CAN MAKE YOU DIZZY

Tomorrow is the deadline for home owners in Massachusetts to install carbon monoxide detectors. I found this installation to be more difficult than I had anticipated.

First thing I did was to try to liberate the device from the clutches of the thick plastic in which it was encased. I tugged on the "open here" tag with enough force to pull the HMS Queen Mary into dock but it wouldn't give. I tried to cut the plastic with a pair of scissors only to have them fold over like a child's rounded-corners primary school scissors.

I got serious and grabbed a pair of lineman's electrical wire cutters from my toolbox and snipped away at the plastic like some mad piranha smelling blood. My wrists ached after five minutes of trying to make an inroad into the plastic. Finally, the plastic sheets separated just enough for me to get two pairs of channel-locking pliers to pull the plastic apart. As the plastic gave way, the alarm plummeted to the floor and three AA batteries fell out and rolled under the couch.

Now that was odd: Not that the batteries rolled under the couch – they always do that – but that there were three batteries, not two. How many devices around the home do you own that require 4.5 volts?

I retrieved the three batteries with a broom handle and with the unsolicited help of our pug dog who finds AA batteries delightfully chewable. I then fished out the instructions. After turning them end-over-end to get to the language with which I am allegedly literate, I followed the directions on battery installation. As soon as I popped in the third battery, mindful of the polarity drawing, the alarm sounded and refused to turn off.

If you have ever experienced 100 decibels of ear-piercing shrieking going off within a foot of your middle-ear tympani, then you can understand the pain I was suffering. I removed a battery to break the circuit and reinserted it. The alarm remained silent.

I cased the hallway for a spot to hang the alarm. It should be close to a bedroom and away from a hamburger-heaven kitchen or diesel-smoking furnace. When I found a spot, I decided to mark the holes to be drilled with a pencil. The instructions said to mount the device "parallel to the hallway." The device is circular. How can you make a circle parallel to anything?

I opted to try to screw in the two screws provided without putting in the plastic expansion plugs. I reasoned that the alarm was very light and the two screws would be able to hold it just fine. I was wrong. The screws fell out instantly when I tried to rotate the alarm onto them for support. So, I got my battery-operated drill and drilled the requisite 3/16-inch holes to accept the expandable inserts.

I took the inserts and tried to push them in with my fingers. They wouldn't budge. I got a hammer and tried to pound them in. They bent over and flattened and became totally useless. This forced me to take out another drill bit and drill the plastic inserts out. The 3/16-inch hole size was growing like a solar eclipse.

I drove to the home improvement store and got a bag of new, slightly larger inserts. This required my drilling new holes and pounding in new inserts.

All the time I kept thinking of my deep exhalations of CO2 next to a CO monitor. My high school chemistry being rusty, I worried that excessive carbon dioxide might confuse a carbon monoxide monitor. After all, what's a molecule of oxygen between friends?

During this whole ordeal I was standing on a three-step plastic step ladder with very narrow steps. I had decided not to use the bigger step ladder, which was located in the Siberia known as my garage. Big mistake. My shins kept bumping the little ladder as I struggled for stability while wielding the electric drill.

Finally, the screws held the anchor plate firmly in place and all I had to do was place the alarm on the screw heads and rotate the device 90 degrees. It wouldn't budge. The screws were too tight. So, I had to take down the plate and loosen the screws just so. Having done this, I tried to rotate the plate on again. It fit with one end hanging down a 1/2 inch more than the other. I took the plate down and readjusted the screws so the plate was level and tight.

One more climb up Everest and I would be able to secure the alarm. Sure enough, my fifth attempt did the trick. The alarm was up and functioning and maybe even parallel to the hallway.

I will have to wait for a geometer to visit my house to verify its position. Until then, I can rest assured that any CO will set off the alarm and get me perpendicular to my bed. I'll try to stay parallel to the hallway as I exit.

61.

WELL, PARTNERS, TIME TO SADDLE UP FOR SPRING

I just finished reading yet another one of Louis L'Amour's Western novels. Despite its hero-always-defeats-bad-guys formula, I loved it. Even 18 years after his death, L'Amour is still the most popular Western writer in the world. His cowboy heroes are strong cunning men who only shoot animals or humans when they deserve it. They champion the wild west in all its native forms and seek to preserve it in its state before railroads, gold strikes and greenhorns.

L'Amour's heroes stretch melodrama to new lows and yet we seem to crave the idea of them. His heroes are rugged men who can sit a saddle for five days straight, draw a six-gun faster than the eye can see, and, oh yeah, read Plutarch at night by their nighttime campfires. No kidding, the hero in the L'Amour novel I just read had only three books in his saddlebags, but one was "Plutarch's Lives" and he read it to find out about leaders and leadership as he lay in his bedroll.

Well, despite the unrealistic multi-dimensionality of his heroes – they're crafty, cunning, strong and brave – my male friends all seem to get crazy just before spring as they try to turn themselves into L'Amour range riders. Most of my friends are prepping their motorcycles, ATVs, fishing boats, tents and camp equipment. They are ready to parachute into spring as soon as a bit of green shows on their lawns.

After watching months of winter beer commercials during televised sporting events, men seem to need to roll out of their recliners and ride the wild prairies or sail the blue waters.

I seem to need to work with rope. After charging my deep-cycle marine battery to power my electric trolling motor for my little bass boat, I find myself coiling and uncoiling rope for the upcoming season. Some lengths I splice to accommodate marine-grade brass snap hooks and others I cut so I can have just the right scope as tie-downs for my canoe that are affixed to the frame under the front and back bumpers of my vehicle.

Now if you are really good at this game, you can spend several full weekends preparing for official L'Amour days. You can polish your kayak, grease the wheels of your trailer, oil the hinges of your garage door (can't have the door binding as you go in and out of the garage to get your outdoor craft ready for the season), waterproof your tent, trim the wick on your lantern, and, in my case, untangle the 16 ropes I use to secure things in the bed of my pickup truck.

I don't know how I developed this pathology for working with rope but it started when I had my first outboard motor-powered boat at age 12. Over the years, I learned some pretty cool knots and seem to seek out situations that call for a rolling bowline or a Prusik knot, which is used for climbing a mast on a sailboat. You've got to know the Prusik if you intend to sail around the Horn.

Or, maybe, I have some as-yet-unrealized desire to be a lariat thrower in the old West and am acting out that fantasy with my rope collection. In addition to the standard stranded ropes I also have some hawsers that I got when I lived in Gloucester by the sea. They are stiff with brine now and are as big as your forearm. These are lines that tugboats use to tow the Queen Mary. I have one hanging up on the wall inside my garage. It weighs about 75 pounds and I have never used it but it adds mightily to the decor of my all-L'Amour-all-the-time garage.

Underneath the hawser is a steel bucket that holds my logging chain. This chain is 20 feet long and has links as big as your wrist (my second anatomical reference today) and has a breaking point that approaches the total weight of my house. I have used this chain to pull out stumps and dislodge boulders. I do wonder what I will do with these heavy items in a few years when I can't sit a saddle for five days or lift 75 pounds easily. Maybe I can get my grand-nephew out from Minnesota and he can haul the hawser and the logging chain out of the garage and toss them into his pickup and drive them out to the state of 10,000 lakes.

About 20 years ago, when I was a newsman in New York City, I had the opportunity to interview the legendary L'Amour. I remember him as a solidly built man with a lot of thick, dark hair and clear, sharp eyes. His grip was strong. I thought about this when I shook his hand and wondered whether his hands were the result of his professional prize-fighting career in which he won 51 of his 59 boxing matches.

He was soft-spoken and had a ready smile. He seemed to want to linger as we finished our interview on the 12th floor of a building just two blocks away from the United Nations and galaxies away from his canyons and mountains. So we sat and talked about air so crisp it snapped and the unending arch of Big Sky country. If I were interviewing him today I might sneak in a question about rope. "Louie, what kind of rope would you choose to corral a 2,000-pound buffalo and what knot would you use, a bowline, a timber hitch?"

A rope for a 2,000-pound buffalo? I'm spending much too much time in my garage.

62.

WHEN TRYING TO FALL ASLEEP IS BUT A DREAM

I received a press release from the American Association for Respiratory Care (AARC) in which they said that "April is a great month to catch up on sleep." Why April? Didn't we just lose an hour springing ahead with Daylight Savings Time? And how about those birds? They're out there in the morning sunlight singing, honking and partying like it was 1999. Who can sleep through that racket?

But seriously, the respiratory therapists say that "Poor sleep quality can have profound effects." Well, we certainly agree with that. One of the effects of no sleep is the huge success of Dunkin' Donuts and Starbucks. Their bottom line is directly proportional to our lack of sleep.

Sleeplessness isn't restricted to Seattle. Most of us spend nights watching the digits turn on our digital clocks: 2:16 becomes 2:17. Even after a trip to the bathroom, the kitchen and the living room, the clock still reads 2:19.

Nothing seems to work to quiet the mind. I try to watch public television. The BBC program, "Battlefield," paradoxically, with warships firing their big guns and Stuka dive bombers shrieking to their targets, often can put me to sleep. It's the soothing British voice of the narrator, who usually has a hyphenated name, like Winston Radcliffe-Brown, that sends me – eventually – into the arms of Morpheus. So does Stacy Keach. He narrates everything: "The big bull elephants stay apart from the females in a loosely organized bachelor herd ... ."

But PBS and Stacy Keach do not always work. Sometimes I get excited about whether the scientists on NOVA will indeed ever find the elusive neutrino or whether the Phoenicians could have survived as an empire longer if they hadn't established Carthage so threateningly close to the Roman Empire.

When television fails, I try to think of tasks that are fun but have lots of steps, like changing the spark plugs and wiring harness on my vehicle's engine. I gather the tools I need in my mind: sparkplug swivel sockets, extensions, wire boot pullers, that special short-handle ratchet that just fits in between the No. 8 plug and the firewall.

Then I think about the removal process and how insanely difficult it is with the anti-air pollution plumbing and electrical harnesses everywhere. I get angry with the engineers who think it is perfectly all right to have to take off the left front wheel to get at the No. 2 plug. "Hey, buddy, get out of your white lab coat and come down here and wrestle with a sparkplug that can only be taken out in arduous, 1/32-of-an-inch turns." This train of thought does not sleep produce.

When ruminating about projects fails, I resort to thinking pleasant pastoral thoughts. I think of being in a canoe and drifting over lily pads on a pond with a slight ripple generated by a Northwest breeze. But often, just as I am gliding over the blue-green water in reverie, a work thought intrudes like a buzzing mosquito: Did I spell the candidate's name right in a headline; did I remember to change 12 percent to 16 percent as so advised in an e-mail from a selectman; did I remember to update a story with a new quote from a voice-mail message?

I toss and turn and the digital numbers march across the clock face like a line of penguins. I've got to remember to buy some tickets to the movies before the penguins leave. But I'm getting too sleepy now to remember that. In the morning I won't recall anything from last night except that I need to do something about my sparkplugs – I think. Or have I changed them already? Can't remember.

"Pour me some more coffee, will you? What's going on out there? Is Hitchcock filming "The Birds" or what?"

63.

NE'ER-DO-WELLS
OF AMERICAN USAGE

One of my bookish readers has urged me to write another column about usage and language peculiarities. I am always reluctant to write about usage because invariably I make a minor but nearly always fatal usage mistake somewhere within the column. It is as if I subconsciously decide to commit some barbarism of language just to give my detractors some forensic evidence to present to the High Court of Rhetoric.

But, here goes. I was talking to my boss the other day who was laying out a special wedding section, and I said, "Always a bridesmaid, never a bride, eh?" I realized after uttering that expression that I didn't really know how it had crept into my bank of idioms. Another phrase, even older is, "He's a hale fellow, well-met." That has a turn of the century (20th century) ring to it.

Speaking of hale, the phrase is "He was haled into court," not hauled into court.

Another ancient phrase is ne'er-do-well, as in constant bad guy. There are many miscreants and laggards who qualify as ne'er-do-wells. Miscreants and laggards have a Captain Bligh tinge to them. I can hear Bligh ordering the laggards to be keelhauled for being ne'er-do-wells.

OK, now don't get angry with me for pointing these out, but here are some other expressions that people often misuse:

Begs the question. Begs the question means avoids the question not prompts the question.

Garnished wages. Unless you work at a farm stand, the correct expression is garnisheed wages, which means to have wages legally deducted and siphoned from your paycheck and given to someone else before you receive them.

Between you and I. Nope. It's between you and me. Between is a preposition and takes the objective case.

Could care less. If you could care less, then you couldn't care less. Use couldn't care less when you mean you have no interest whatsoever.

Runs the gambit. You mean runs the gamut, which means a wide array. Also, don't confuse gamut with gauntlet. If you have to run a gauntlet, be prepared to take some blows.

One hundred and 10 percent. This may be appropriate talk when you are behind the looking glass with Alice in some multi-dimensional universe, but here in the Real World, 100 percent, like the speed of light, is the maximum percentage the gods of mathematics allow us.

Road closure. Unless you are living on Psychology Lane, the appropriate word is closing. Closure is a pop psychology word used to mean an emotional resolution and ending. This is not to be confused with cloture, which means, according to Webster's dictionary, "the closing or limitation of debate in a legislative body especially by calling for a vote."

Let me close with Shakespeare, who single-handedly invented more phrases and expressions than any human. Everyone knows his famous "To be, or not to be" soliloquy in "Hamlet" but many forget the other famous lines coupled with the To be ones:

To be, or not to be: that is the question;
Whether 'tis nobler in the mind to suffer
The slings and arrows of outrageous fortune,
Or to take arms against a sea of troubles,
And by opposing end them?

May you escape the slings and arrows of outrageous usage and may your sea of troubles be caught by your spell checker.

64.

CHARLIE AND THE POWER OF POOKIES

I spent about 10 minutes with my new friend Charlie recently and I felt much better thanks to his visit. Charlie has a magical effect on my mood. Even when I am down below periscope depth and rigged for depth charges, a mere smile from Charlie empties the bilge from my emotional ballast and sends me to the sunny surface.

You see, Charlie is 9 months old and looks like a Renaissance painting of a cherub. Although I do admit that in his woolen cap and storm gear, he sometimes looks a little like a Russian ambassador in miniature. Either way, he could coax a smile out of a curmudgeon. So pervasive is his power of innocence.

During a recent visit, Charlie rode into the newsroom bouncing on his mother's hip. He looked at all the lights and colorful computer screens but was content in the end to nibble on a cell phone that his mother had given him to keep him entertained. He understood the phone had something to do with the mouth but has as yet not discovered the wonders of speaking wirelessly. May that discovery not arrive until his teenage years.

When he grew tired of the cell phone, he held his hands together like Pope John Paul in Vatican Square. Little did he know that he was giving us the special blessing that only babies are empowered to deliver: Go and have hope, for how can such utter innocence exist if the future is not based on hope and good will. The innocence of babes is indeed a universality among all peoples and all cultures.

As parents, we all have seen that smile in our children that makes us want to hug them and protect them, now and forever. Even when they are grown, on their own, and moved away, we still hope that they are happy and smiling. We know that no matter how successful we are, how high are own worldly trajectory is, it is for naught if our children are unhappy or having bad days.

And there will be bad days in every life. Small and big things will happen: a child will not get a spot on an athletic team or do badly on an exam, be betrayed by a former friend or be taunted by cruel kids.

Later on in their adult lives they will witness and even be a part of tragedy — lose a loved one or lose one's own health or suffer a reversal of fortune.

That is why the precious Charlies of the world bridge all gaps among us and with their pookie smiles help us remember those blessed times when our children were happy and content to play peek-a-boo, and perhaps later as a finale, chew on a cell phone, and smile.

65.

IS DAVE BARRY HYPHENATED?

Editors worry. It is the nature of the job. When you are trying to tell a story accurately under the pressure of deadline, mistakes invariably occur. But we all know about the macro aspects of reporting the news — the need to be factual, unbiased, relevant, fast. But after years of being an editor, one worries about things that might seem so small they are subatomic.

For example, I worry about this - , a hyphen. I get upset if a story I have edited contains a hyphen in a word structure like "strongly worded statement." There should be no hyphen because "strongly" is an adverb modifying an adjective. So in all the pages of the newspaper, with all the millions of letters and symbols, I worry about one too many - (hyphens).

I also worry that I will make some grammatical mistake in this very column about how I hate grammatical mistakes. I will run this through the spell checker and the grammar checker that Microsoft provides with every Windows-based PC and then I will have a fellow editor proof-read this column. (I don't know why that should bring me any solace. Doesn't he ask me to proof-read *his* articles and don't I always find at least one error in them?) (By the way, I checked the Oxford English Dictionary and proof-read as a verb takes a hyphen.)

Am I worrying too much? Can an editor worry too much? Now I am worrying that the reader will think I squander my worried-ness (is there such a word and does it contain a hyphen?). Worry about the big things, I hear them say. Well, I worry about those a lot — hundreds of times more than I worry about a - .

I worry randomly. I worry about a comment I heard in the newsroom about another column writer. The comment was that the other columnist was trying too much to be like Dave Barry, the Miami-based, Pulitzer Prize-winning humor writer. (How about *those* hyphens, eh?) Well, for the record, I was writing columns more than a decade before Dave Barry started writing his newspaper columns. I know that sounds like a putdown and I mean it to be, but I admit he is funnier than I am, has a lot more hair and probably more hyphens at his disposal. (Now that off-the-shoulder shot will generate some e-mails from Barry fans.) I worry about e-mails, not because they take a hyphen, which they do, but because they often contain enough venom to qualify as a weapon of mass destruction.

But, all seriousness aside, as comedian Steve Allen used to say, (I used the word comedian because my readers are so young they probably have never heard of Steve Allen), one cannot write a newspaper column without holding opinions and sometimes those opinions are held by others only when they are wearing rubber gloves. (An aside: how many rubber gloves do the casts of "CSI" and "CSI Miami" use each week?)

I'm going to send this column to Dave Barry to see what he thinks about hyphens and rubber gloves. Do they use either in Miami — I mean other than the cast of "CSI Miami?"

I have to close now. I'm worried that I won't make my deadline and that my headline (still to be written) won't be clever enough. I bet Dave Barry hires people to write his headlines.

ABOUT THE AUTHOR

Peter Costa is a veteran journalist who has worked for weekly and daily newspapers, national magazines, and an international wire service. He covered the United Nations and interviewed four U.S. presidents and has the stolen stationery and ashtray to prove it.

He is a senior editor for the Community Newspaper Company and is the editor of the Westford Eagle and the Bedford Minuteman. He lives in Massachusetts with his wife and daughter. He loves his Pug dog, Grace, and discusses national politics with her every night.